MURDER IN THE MARSHES

A BLAKE SISTERS TRAVEL MYSTERY – BOOK 4

CARTER FIELDING

Published by Carter Fielding Press
5237 River Road, #304
Bethesda, MD 20216

Editing, design, and distribution by Bublish, Inc.

ISBN: 978-1-647045-65-4 (eBook)
ISBN: 978-1-647045-66-1 (paperback)

**For information about the author and her projects
please visit:
www.mcarterfielding.com**

PROLOGUE

HE WASN'T DEAD WHEN HE was stuffed into the closet, but he knew he was dying. The incessant ringing in his ears, the blurriness of his vision that wasn't blocked by the blood dripping down his face and catching in his beard, the resounding waves of pain that crashed into the sides of his skull—all were signs of his impending fate. What little breath he could catch was stifled by the closeness of the closet and the sack that surrounded him. There was a strange calmness that wove itself in between the spasms of survival, forcing his brain to focus on how to untie the sack, push his body toward the shaft of light that crept under the door, overcome the pain, and finally, simply endure it.

In the end, his mental strength zapped long after his physical stamina had surrendered. His thoughts wandered as his life ebbed. All the things he wanted to do flashed through his mind—climbing Kilimanjaro and seeing the Great Migration across the Maasai Mara, taking a boat trip along the Nile, following the path of his ancestors to Charleston, painting the upstairs bathroom, and fixing the crumbling stacked stone back wall in his garden. The to-do list faded into his bucket list. *Why do they call it a bucket list?* he wondered. Things to do before you kicked the bucket? He would have laughed if half his spirit hadn't already left his body. The lists didn't matter. Neither one would ever get done.

So, this is what it feels like when you die, he thought. He succumbed to the thought before his body fully yielded to the reality of dying. His eyes fixed on the pattern at the edge of the curtain, all that he could see through the crack under the door. If he could only reach it, be sure that it was real, he might survive. His arm jutted upward in a final defiance. *Touch it. You're not gone yet. If you can feel it, you're not gone.* Yet he knew he was going. His final thought was that he should have gone home. If he had just gone home . . .

1

HOME. THE NOTION OF "HOME" had never struck her like it did when Max said it. Maybe it was the newness of him back in her life. Maybe it was the fear that what he called "home" might be different from what she had in mind. Whatever it was, Finley Blake paused when Max asked if she was excited to be heading home.

"What is the first thing you'll do when you get home?" asked Max Davies, her partner in life for the last ten months and for the next hundred years, as they talked about the plans for her sister's wedding in Charleston that was only four weeks away.

They were sitting in their mews house in Chelsea on a raw April morning. It had taken Finley a little while to get used to calling it "their" house. In her mind, it had always been "Max's" house. He had owned it when they'd been together seven years ago in Tangier and when they'd split some two years later. He had still owned it when they'd reconnected in Tangier, almost two years ago to the day.

It hadn't become "theirs" until several months ago, when he had stood in the study just down the hall from where they now sat, during Whitt's engagement party, and slipped the spectacular diamond, yellow and white gold band on her finger. He had pledged his everlasting love and asked her to join him on an endless journey through life. It hadn't been a marriage, but rather a life commitment. Max had a thing about marriage. When he had explained his aversion to the institution, Finley had understood. She wasn't in love with marriage. She was desperately, and forever, in love with him. So, they had settled into blissful cohabitation in "committed permanence without marriage."

Max brought her mental wanderings back to the present. "When I was traveling and would finally get back here—home— my first thing was a whiskey in the back garden. I'd drop my bag at the stairs, grab my mail, select a single malt, and head to the garden—even in the rain. The mist was never heavy with the cover of the trees."

His voice trailed off, and Finley looked at him, deep in his reminiscence of that first taste of home. Finley had to think about what she did first when she walked through the door, back from a trip. To a degree, it depended on where she had landed at the end of the voyage. When she was in New York, before she and Max had firmly taken root together and she had transplanted herself in London, she would order Thai or Lebanese from her favorite take-out place on Amsterdam, even before her shoes were off. Then she would pour herself a glass of wine and flip through the mound of mail that had accumulated in the weeks she'd been gone.

If she was in Chevy Chase, camping at Mama and Daddy's on the return leg, she would get deposited at the kitchen island on a stool, with an elegant flute of champagne or prosecco in front of her, while Daddy took her bag upstairs to her room and Mama finished putting dinner together. Since she had been in London with Max, she had followed his patterns, not yet establishing a "welcome home" rhythm that was uniquely her own.

"I don't know. I guess it depends," Finley finally responded. Max stood to refill her mug with the Ugandan blend she'd brought back from a reconnaissance trip to East and Central Africa a few weeks before. "Coffee or wine figures significantly into the equation wherever home is at the time and whenever I get there."

"But isn't there something that you miss? That you think about the longer you're away, as you get more homesick? That shows up in your dreams, that you can taste on your tongue?" Max got more animated as he threw out each question, as if to provoke her mind into remembering something. Anything.

Finley watched him warm to the subject. His eyes widened as he spoke, and his lips met, as if tasting something memorable, something evocative of the tastes and smells that assured him he was finally home. She smiled, enjoying his excitement. Yet, she still shook her head. "Nope. Nothing comes to mind. Nothing that happens every time I get back from a trip. Heck, most of the time, I don't even know where home is. Sometimes New York, sometimes with you in Delhi or here in London, sometimes in DC, sometimes in Charleston. I'll have to think about it."

"Interesting," was all Max said, as he scanned her face. After a minute, he leaned down and brushed his lips on hers before returning to kiss her fully. "Home is where the heart is, so they say. Where is your heart, darling?"

"Wherever you are," she murmured quietly, tilting her head to look up at him and catching the chiseled angle of his jaw in the filtered light. "And therein lies the trouble. Since you—we—are everywhere." She took his face in her hands and traveled its plains and valleys with her eyes. She traced her thumbs along the laugh lines that framed his mouth before embracing his lips with hers.

When they parted, Max studied her eyes in return. Eventually he spoke. "So, what's the plan for next month? I know your mother has an agenda that we are to follow. I also know that you have work to do before we head to Charleston, so fill me in."

"The most important thing for me right now is prepping for this trip to Tanzania. I'm so glad they brought me back in to do the follow-up on the story we did last year."

Finley reached over and tore off the end of the almond croissant Max had just put on his plate. She put one crusty horn on the edge of her napkin and then leaned over to tear off the other end. Max sipped his coffee as he watched her work. They had long ago agreed to this division of eating labor, since Max liked the soft innards of most foods and Finley liked the crispy outsides. It worked for most things they ate. They had yet to come across anything where they both reached for the same portion. She popped a sliced almond into her mouth. "The backstory on the shift in the great migration cycles because of climate change is a nice angle for the piece that *Traveler's Tales* is doing. And a documentary, too. A nice departure."

"Where are you going to be?" Max munched on his piece of the croissant. "And when do you leave again?"

"I leave at the end of next week and will only be gone for a couple of weeks," Finley relayed. "I'll be flying into Arusha but then taking a prop into Serengeti National Park. I may head over to the crater," she said, referring to the Ngorongoro Crater, an ancient caldera that was home to leopards, black rhinos, and lions.

She continued, "I'll come back here, though, before we go. We'll have a few days before we head to South Carolina. I'll need to repack. My mother would not appreciate me showing up for a wedding—a Southern wedding no less—with only boots and khakis in my bag!"

Max chortled at the imaginary look of disgust and dismay on Mama's face if field gear had been Finley's only attire. "Are all the women in your family as persnickety as your mother?"

"Well, I'm not, and Whitt isn't."

"You, no. But Whitt can be a little high-maintenance, you have to admit," Max reminded her gently. He waited for her reaction.

Finley grinned. "Yes. The girl can be a handful at times." She thought for a moment. "Quite honestly, the Blake *and* Montgomery women—and you'll get to meet both sides—run the gamut. Some are easygoing, others are prickly. And others can be downright rude in that subtle, Southern way. Most all of us are obstinate and opinionated, even the ones that look like shrinking violets. Don't let that facade fool you. The term 'steel magnolias' was created for a reason—to describe Southern women."

Max slipped behind her and draped his arms around her shoulders. "Is my darling girl admitting to being a little bullheaded at times?"

"Only when necessary." She turned and planted a kiss on his chin. "Only when wholly necessary."

Max returned to his side of the island and began clearing away the dishes. "So, what do you have planned for the rest of the day? I have some project RFPs I need to review. My year of following after you will be over before we know it, and I need to have some consulting work to go back to."

"I need to look at the Serengeti contact sheets from last year to see which of those photos I can use, and then I need to scope out the storyline I want to try. That should take me until next week!" Finley rose and moved her mug to the dishwasher. "Or at least until dinner."

Max chuckled. "It won't be that bad if you focus."

"That's a big if."

"So we don't have to worry about dinner, let's go out. And I'll find a place, so you don't even have to think of that."

Finley went to Max and wrapped her arms around him. "You are just too good to me!" She released him with a peck on his cheek before heading upstairs to her study.

When she had moved in, Max had wanted to give up a portion of his downstairs study for her so they could work in proximity to each other. After a few days, in which his conference calls had disrupted her concentration while writing, she had quietly moved her things to the smaller of the spare bedrooms upstairs. He hadn't said anything. Rather, he made periodic trips up the stairs to check on her, often saying nothing during his passage down the hall, but always sticking his head in to glance at her as she worked.

Finley opened her computer and started scrolling through the contact sheets. Page upon page of the animals, people, and scenery that the earlier camera crew had shot almost seven months earlier came to life on the screen. She hadn't been in Tanzania to see the migration, having been called in at the last minute as backup to cover the Zanzibar leg after the principal team had been pulled to film a tiger trek in India. She and Max had used it as a mini-honeymoon, since the Zanzibar trip had come shortly after they'd committed to each other.

Finley took the opportunity now to carefully examine each frame on the sheet and take in the powerful stories that had been frozen in time. Sam, the principal photographer for the shoot, had marked the frames that she liked best, providing a caption for most of them in addition to the date and location. As Finley located a pre-ferred shot among the numerous photos on a page, she would glance at the ten or so shots before and after to see whether she agreed with Sam's assessment. Sam's eye was so attuned to light and color that there were often as many as three or four great shots to choose from. In that instance, Finley went for either the one that had the greatest action or the one that told the most compelling story.

Even though the timing of her trip would be too early to catch the wildebeest crossing of the Mara River that most associate with the great migration, Finley was looking forward to spending the latter part of the calving season in Serengeti National Park with the park staff—the rangers, vets, trackers, and guides who balanced the preferences of the tourists, who were the financial fuel of the park, with the needs of the animals and terrain that were its lifeblood.

Traveler's Tales had decided that the time was right for a con-versation around climate change and its impact on tourism. Dan Burton, her editor at the magazine and a former law school class-mate, had selected Finley to capture the story at both Serengeti and Maasai Mara. Other teams were being dispatched to Kodiak National Wildlife Refuge in Alaska, Yala National Park in Sri Lanka, the Great Barrier Reef in Australia, and several other lo-cations around the world to film portions of a documentary the magazine was compiling. It was new territory for the magazine, a departure from its print format, but no less hard-hitting than some of its other stories on identity theft and human trafficking. Finley had contributed significantly to the latter story.

Her concentration was broken by the ringing of her cellphone and the picture of her sister Whitt's face popping up on her screen.

"Hey, kid. What's up?" Finley asked. "Where are you?"

"Mumbai still. The project is delayed a few weeks, but I should be able to make it to Charleston without too much hassle. David is flying into Doha from Tbilisi, and we'll meet there. We'll see you at home at the end of the month."

"You sound pretty casual about making it home for the wedding. You sure the delays won't trip you up? You and David are pretty important players." Finley surveyed her sister's face on the screen. She seemed calm and normal, but with Whitt, it was hard to tell. The hotel could be on fire and Whitt would continue the conversation as if nothing were amiss. "Everything all right? You guys aren't getting cold feet, are you?"

"No, we're okay. David is a little nervous about meeting the whole clan, but I told him if it gets too much, we'll just grab you and Max and head off to the justice of the peace." Whitt paused for effect. "Or Vegas! We never wanted a big wedding anyway."

"Mama would kill you! She's been working her tuchus off for this wedding. And whether you want it or not, she's going to have it, even if she has to kidnap you two to get you there!" Finley laughed at the thought of Whitt and David being carried down the aisle with gunnysacks over their heads and dropped at the altar. *Don't mess with Mama, girl. It'll get ugly, and there is no way you're going to win!*

"I know. But I refuse to stress over this project or my wedding. So, the Reserve Bank of India's delays are not going to ruffle me. Nor is David's request to add more fraternity brothers to the guest list. Even Mama questioning my decision not to wear a veil isn't going to get a reaction."

"That's the attitude. This is your wedding, and you call the shots." Finley knew how it would go down. Whitt would state her preferences. Mama would purse her lips before giving a radiant smile, nodding her head in agreement—and then she would go off and do whatever she darn well pleased.

"When do you and Max get in? And thank you so much for suggesting and arranging the Airbnb in town, instead of us staying on Sullivan's Island." Whitt sighed. "I love what Mama and all are doing for us, but that house is going to be crazy and all the questions and suggestions and such would just send me around the bend. If I'm not there already."

"It will give us a little time together, too. Max and I will run interference with Mama, so don't worry. She's just excited. This is the only chance she's going to get to do this wedding thing."

"You and Max still aren't ever going to jump the broom?"

"Nope. We're happy with the way things are. I understand how the trauma from his parents' divorce soured him on marriage. But it didn't sour him on commitment. We're no less married than if we had gone to the courthouse."

"I know and Mama and Daddy understand, but be prepared for whispering at the house." Whitt shook her head. "Tongues'll be wagging."

"And I'll just redirect them back your way. This is your day, and nothing is going to mar that!" Finley beamed at her sister. "In only a month, you and David will be married! Who'd have thunk it, kid!"

"Not me. I figured I'd be the last one to walk down the aisle and that you surely would've. You can never tell!"

"Speaking of not telling . . . Mama still hasn't figured out that you switched the guest list she sent to the calligrapher?" Finley stared at Whitt through the screen, her eyes wide. "How the heck did you pull that off? More importantly, what are you going to say when she discovers it?"

"'Sorry, I must have pulled the wrong file?'" Whitt snickered under her breath before letting loose her indignation. "She had fifth cousins twice removed on there who we haven't seen in a month of Sundays! It's bad enough I have to put up with having Cousin

Tommy and Lael there, plus all of the cousins on Daddy's side. I told her I wanted a small wedding, and that is something I won't surrender on."

"Well, you may win on this one. It would be inappropriate to send out invitations this late. Mama will just have to suck it up."

Whitt chuckled again. "Yep, that she will. Look, before I forget what I called you for . . . it's about Evans. Is there space in the house for him to stay a couple of nights? He will be coming in the night of the rehearsal dinner and leaving on Sunday, so it literally is just a couple of nights. I'd like to accommodate him if we can."

Chief Inspector Gareth Evans, an Interpol agent who had recently been promoted, had on more than one occasion saved the sisters' necks. That said, they had returned the favor in Sri Lanka, rescuing him from certain death. After all they had been through together, it seemed wrong not to invite him to the wedding.

"The house has seven bedrooms and a study, so even with Charlie, Kirsten and Reid, Logan and Hema, and Mooney and her new beau, there is more than enough room." Finley enumerated. "And then we rented the other house on Montagu, too, and that one has five rooms and a sleeping porch. I don't think it's booked up with the Blake cousins yet. There is more than enough space."

"What about Max?"

"What about him? He'll be fine with it," Finley smirked. "And, if he's not, he can sleep on the couch! It was crazy in the first place that he ever thought there was anything between Evans and me. If he is still jealous after all this time, he needs to check himself."

"Easier said than done with Max. That man guards you like Fort Knox. I'm just trying to head off potential issues before they happen. I'd hate for guests to come to blows at my wedding."

Finley snorted with laughter. "That would never happen with those two. Evans is too buttoned-up British, and Max would never allow himself to lose control like that. Nah, they might glare at each other, but they'd never duke it out. And over what? That storm passed long ago."

"I hope so. Then it's settled. Evans is in the Rutledge house with all of us. I'd better get going. Got a list a mile long of things I need to take care of. Thanks loads. Love you. And love to Max."

"Back at you. Love to David. See you in a few weeks!"

When Finley put the phone down, Max was standing at the door, smiling. "I knew it sounded like too much fun up here for you to be working! How's Whitt doing? Got a case of nerves?"

"No, she's really calm, which I should've expected. She may toss her cookies before she walks down the aisle, but nary a guest will ever know." Finley decided to lob the Evans grenade and see how it landed. "She wanted to know if there was room in our house for Evans to stay a few nights. I told her I thought we could fit him in."

Max stood next to her, his eyes on the shot she had just pulled up of a lion bringing down a wildebeest. He tapped the screen. "Nice shot! On Evans, sure. If there's room. Goodness knows you two owe the man your lives. And on more than one occasion!"

"Thanks, babe! That's one thing off my chest." Finley exhaled.

"What? You thought I would object? Why?"

"Well, the two of you have never exactly been BFFs!"

"Acknowledged, but hey, I won the girl, so no hard feelings." He claimed his prize with a thorough kiss that left her a little light-headed. "You ready for dinner? We have reservations in an hour, but if now isn't a good time for you to stop, I can move them."

"Nope, this is perfect timing. I just finished creating my final card. I'll take a few clean memory cards just in case I want a different mix, but this will get me started." Finley turned off the computer and closed it. "Where are we heading?"

"A surprise!"

The surprise turned out to be Le Colombier, one of her favorite restaurants, a modern bistro on the edge of their neighborhood. For reasons she couldn't remember, they hadn't visited it since they'd returned from Delhi. Max beamed as she recognized the direction they were walking and squeezed his hand in anticipation.

"Thank you! I had almost forgotten about this little place."

"I'm glad you still like it." Max kissed her forehead as they neared the entrance. "Maybe this can be *our* 'welcome home' routine. We'll drop the bags and head here, to a table in the back corner, and decompress. I'll have my single malt here with you, in the back garden if it's warm or at the back table if it's too cold."

"Done. What a lovely new tradition!" Finley grinned as she settled into her seat. They were seated at a table inside since the April evening had turned chilly. She'd thrown on a black, midi-length ribbed-knit dress, with a blush blazer and strappy, black kitten heels, not knowing exactly how upscale they were going. Max hadn't given her any clues when he'd pulled on a pair of charcoal trousers, his signature marine-blue shirt, and a blue-and-green houndstooth jacket. He wasn't in jeans, but with what he had on, he could have been going to an afternoon gallery opening, with the addition of a tie and pocket square, or down the street to his favorite wine shop to place another order. *Men's clothing is so ambiguous! At times like this, I need Mooney to help style me,* Finley had thought as she'd gotten dressed.

Sitting there now, though, it didn't matter. Max, looking at her like she hung the moon, made her feel regal, whether she had on a tiara or cutoffs. She marveled at how close they had come to walking away from each other forever. How this creating of their special traditions might never have happened.

"What are you thinking?" Max reached across the table and took her hand in his. "You look awfully pensive. That scares me!"

"Does it? Why? What do you think I'm going to say? If I'm unhappy or puzzled, I've learned to put the issue on the table rather than pocket it." *A realization that might have saved a lot of heartache if it had come earlier, eh, girlfriend?* "And right now, I'm deliriously happy!"

"Are you?" Max sat back in his chair and watched her face break into a grin that had the corners of her eyes dancing. "What are you so happy about?"

"Everything! Being here with you, heading to Tanzania, Whitt and David getting married, seeing my family."

"Tell me about this family of yours. I've met your parents and heard a bit about your cousin, Odessa, but tell me about some of the others."

Finley took a slow sip of her Riesling. It was dry and surprisingly full-bodied, with the aromatic fruitiness she liked. If she had wine at any of her family's houses, except Mama and Daddy's, it was likely to be sweet like the iced tea. She would have to warn Max to stick to beer or bourbon.

What could she tell him about her family that wouldn't overwhelm him or scare him off? There would be a lot of them, that was for sure, since both sides would be coming, and that meant extended as well as immediate family. She thought back on all the times the Sullivan's Island house had been overrun with family, usually for weddings or funerals. Those were the times everyone felt compelled to make a showing. While the adults talked or cooked, or talked while they cooked, the kids, all cousins by blood or friendship, would play tag or red-light-green-light in the expansive backyard, which would soon be decorated for Whitt's wedding.

Her mind wandered back to one of those summers. Finley had been about twelve or thirteen, and Whitt six or so. They had slipped away from the rest of the pack and headed up the stairs that led to the widow's walk circling the uppermost level of the house. They had wanted to see the water that was visible from both the front and the back of that level—the ocean on the front side and the marshes on the back. They had only been on the deck for a few minutes when they heard snickering and saw the hatch door drop. Before they could reach it, the door slammed shut. They heard the bolt engage and knew they were locked out. The noise of all the people on the porch and in the yard muffled their cries for help, and after a few minutes, they sat and watched as the sun slipped below the horizon and night started to creep in. When Daddy found them some time later, Finley had used the skirt of her dress to cover her sister and was singing her to sleep.

Daddy was merciless in his punishment of the perpetrators. He never said a word, but when dessert—a humungous chocolate layer cake and homemade vanilla bean ice cream—was passed around that evening, Daddy made sure that the miscreants were skipped. His glare dared them to protest. Finley never did forgive Lael and Tommy for that prank. She wasn't sure she ever would.

2

"**Y**ou almost ready to head to the airport?" David Quinn, soon-to-be husband of Whitt and brother-in-law of Finley, fixed his eyes on the blurry screen image that periodically froze before doing a pixelated catch-up a few seconds later. "Where are you? The connection is horrible!"

"I'm on the terrace of the apartment. The internet doesn't really reach out here, but I wanted to put the plants out so they get a bit of water in case Vandana forgets to look after them." Whitt swung the camera around so David could see what she was doing.

She generally stayed in corporate apartments rather than hotels if her assignment in a country was going to be more than a couple of weeks. In this case, the project had run several months, with a few breaks in between. There'd been delays that had kept her in Mumbai longer than she wanted, but now she was packed up and ready to leave. The time had gone faster than she'd expected. She was heading home to Charleston to get married! This place was the apartment manager Vandana's responsibility now.

Whitt turned the camera back around. "I'm walking out the door in a few minutes, but I thought I'd check in with you while I waited."

"Miss me that much or afraid I was going to do a runner and miss the flight?" David chuckled.

"Missed you, I guess." Whitt sighed. "Maybe we both can do a runner and just skip the wedding. Finley said she and Max would cover for us."

"What, you mean walk down the aisle in our place?" David's eyes widened in surprise. "I'm almost tempted to bug out on our wedding just to see that!"

"No, they'd never do that! You know Max and marriage. Nah, just delay Mama—less so Daddy—so we could get away!"

David's voice softened. "You're really that scared? If so, we can go to the courthouse and be done with it. I don't care. I just want to be with you. Forever. Whatever it takes for that to happen is all right with me."

"Not scared, really. Just afraid I'm going to be overwhelmed by the goings-on."

"Just stick with me, then. If you're feeling like you're drowning, I'll whisk you away until you feel grounded again."

"That's why I love you—you always have my back!"

"And your front, and your middle, and all the parts in between! I love you. Always have!"

"Love you, too. Look, I'd better go. The taxi's outside. See you in a few hours. For that, I can't wait!"

"See you in a few, babe. Love you so much." David planted a kiss on his fingertip and transferred it to the screen, where Whitt received it and sent one of her own in return.

Whitt stared at the screen until it faded to black and a picture of David, one from their early days in Morocco, came up as the screensaver. *A few more hours and I get to touch him instead of a screen. And in a few more days, I get to have him in my life for always!* She gathered her bags and continued grinning at that last thought all the way down the hall and into the cab.

"This place is phenomenal! Finley outdid herself this time." Whitt was wandering around the ground floor of the classic Georgian house—what was commonly called a Charleston single—they had rented for their stay in Charleston. While staying in the family house on Sullivan's Island would have had memories for the sisters, the thought of being in the vortex of all the wedding preparation chaos prompted Finley to book two houses within a block of each other for the wedding party and younger guests, mainly the cousins, who would be coming into town. Best of all, the houses were in the heart of the city, so it would be easy to distract Whitt with a gin tasting or carriage ride if she got a case of the wedding jitters.

Whitt and David had flown into Charleston from Atlanta that morning, after spending a getaway night in Georgia. David had made use of the layover time after the flight from Doha to head into downtown Atlanta and meet with some potential clients for several Moldovan and Georgian wines he was introducing into the American market. He'd suggested they change their Charleston flight from the evening to the morning and then surprised Whitt by reserving the Astor Suite at the St. Regis Atlanta that night.

"You had this all planned, didn't you?" Whitt said, as she was ushered into the suite. The champagne, Pol Roger Sir Winston Churchill, was on ice, and a large bouquet of passion-pink peonies was on the table. "This wasn't a 'last-minute change because the meeting ran over' was it?"

David stood near the door, grinning as Whitt stared at him in wonder. "I wanted you to myself before all the festivities got started." He walked over and put his arms around her waist. "I figured this was as good a way as any. I guess it worked. Though, I did think for a moment there that you were going to overrule me!"

The next morning, they caught the forty-five-minute flight to Charleston and drove straight to the Rutledge Avenue house. Now, they were here, in Charleston, steeling themselves for the onslaught of family mayhem, wedding obligations, and pasted-on smiles.

"Let's go get some breakfast and wander around before we head over to Sullivan's," Whitt said. "I told Mama not to expect us until after dinner. Finley and Max will be here by then, and we can face the mob together!"

"Now you really have me scared. The fact that you want reinforcements before you make an entrance is a bit troubling." David's brow creased, but the ends of his mouth quirked upward slightly.

"They're not all that bad." Whitt paused. "Well, not all of them!" She laughed and gave David a light peck on the lips. "Let's go get you fortified for battle, my gallant warrior!"

They headed down Rutledge Avenue along the lake until they reached Queen and then cut across to King Street. The day was seasonably bright, with a sweet breeze that carried the scents of gardenias, honeysuckle, and jasmine. Every house along the street was decorated for spring with dogwood, jonquil, and hyacinth blossoms abounding.

"Is Charleston always this pretty or did we just catch it in the best season?" David asked.

"It's always this pretty. Just a different kind of pretty in each season. Camelias in the winter. All of this in the spring. Lilacs and cutting flowers in the summer. And then marigolds, petunias, and mums in the fall."

"A gardener's delight! But you never struck me as the gardening type." David glanced over at Whitt as they walked, hand in hand, up the street. "I've never seen you with dirt under your nails."

"And I dare say you won't. That's Finley's cup of tea. She doesn't mind getting her hands dirty. In fact, I think she rather likes it," Whitt declared. "But Southern girls don't have to plant to know what grows and when."

"So I'm learning. I don't mind a little dirt, so just let me know what you want planted and when."

"And where! We need to figure out where we're going to live once we're married. We keep skirting around it, but if we don't decide soon, you'll still be in Tbilisi and I'll be in Manila. And I don't think that is going to work for long," Whitt said.

They reached the entrance to Millers All Day, an upscale diner noted for its biscuits, country ham, and grits. There was a short line out the door. David moved forward to put their name on the waiting list before returning to Whitt.

"Only a fifteen-minute wait. I think I'll survive." David was known for his perpetual appetite. Whitt had gotten him a biscuit and coffee before they got on the plane, but she knew that had worn off a while ago. She wondered how far into their marriage it would be before the buff surfer boy she married became a soft, pudgy Pillsbury Doughboy. Whenever it happened, she would love him still, just as deeply.

David continued, "So back to a home location. What are you thinking?"

"I want to stay with the bank a little longer. I like the work, especially the ability to travel to the clients and work with them on developing the projects, and I have a fair bit of flexibility. That said, Manila is not where I want to be buried. But unless I can find a slot in one of the field offices, I think we may be stuck there as our official home base."

"That may not be so bad. You still have projects in Tbilisi. India is winding down, but you talked about other work in Uzbekistan, which you can get to fairly easily from Georgia."

"So, are you saying we continue this long-distance craziness?" Whitt's voice was tight, and sadness entered her eyes.

David ignored the hostess when she called their name. Instead, he reached over and took Whitt's face in his hands. "No. Just hear me out. Once we're seated, I'll explain." He kissed her gently before responding to the summons to eat.

After the waitress took their order and brought their drinks—a gin Lemon Drop for Whitt and a Gullah Cream Ale for David—David resumed the conversation. "What I was attempting to say was that we should probably keep both apartments for now. You need the Manila base even though you'll rarely be there. And you can use the Tbilisi place as your working base for the projects in Georgia and Uzbekistan."

Whitt's expression said she was unconvinced. "But where will you be?"

"With you, wherever you are." David stroked her cheek gently. "Most of the distribution arrangements have been worked out, and I have people in place—or I will in the next couple of months—to execute them. So, I can be any place in the world and make it work."

"You sure? I don't want all the work you've put into this to fall apart because you took your eye off the ball."

"Won't happen. I probably couldn't have done this a year ago, but we're in a good place now, and I can step back a little and focus on marketing."

Whitt let a sad little breath escape. In its place, a smile slid up her lips. She took a slow sip of her drink and let it linger on her tongue. *He's been thinking about this. About us. I thought I was the only one fretting. I worried myself sick for nothing! He's a keeper! He'd better be, or Mama would kill us!*

"You okay with that?" David probed, trying to see if his thinking was solid. He waited, his eyes searching her face for a sign. When he got the nod, he smiled and raised his glass. "I hoped you would be. Here's to our next chapter. I can't wait!"

Whitt slowly started to untangle the mass of emotions that had been balled up in her stomach. Now that she could breathe, she might be able to eat something. She'd been craving biscuits and country ham since they'd touched down, and Millers took the humble, poor man's sandwich to another level with the dollop of fig preserve and the slice of Havarti they added. David lasered in on the steak and eggs—with a side of soft, cushiony waffles—and was now savoring his first bite with closed eyes and a look of rapture.

Having averted what she thought might have been a crisis, Whitt took the time now to look around the room. The restaurant was full, but the stream of people flowing in had stemmed a bit and the noise level had lessened enough that she and David could talk at normal decibels. The wooden floors and bleached-wood walls absorbed a lot of the sound and gave it a warm buzz. In the center of the room, the rich browns of the wood high tables and accents were offset with bright aqua-and-gray metal chairs, giving it an eclectic vibe that defied categorization.

"I like this place. We can have breakfast here every morning!" David exclaimed, as they exited onto the street after finishing their meals.

"There're a lot of places here that serve breakfast like this. Toast. Or Callie's. Or Bitty and Beau's," Whitt mused. "Why don't we try a few other places for lunch or coffee and see what you think then? Charleston is a foodie's playground, so you'll never go hungry or without a topnotch meal."

"My kind of city! Where to now?"

"I need to walk some of this food down, so let's wander along the water and then go unpack. By that time, I'll be ready for a quick nap before Finley and Max get in."

"Sounds good to me. Lead on!"

Whitt laid out a planned course that took them out to the pier at Ravenel Waterfront Park and around the Battery before turning across Broad and back to the Rutledge Avenue house. On the way, they might amble past the art galleries that peppered Queen Street and check out a few shops on King and Meeting Street, especially the bookstore at the Preservation Society of Charleston. If they weren't running too far behind, they might pop in for a tour of one of the historic homes on the East Battery. Then maybe they'd take time to people watch in White Point Garden before heading toward Colonial Lake again and then home. She would have to figure out how to add in Rainbow Row and St. Philip's Church cemetery. Maybe she would just leave those for the carriage tours that Finley and Mama had planned for the wedding party later in the week.

Within the itinerary Whitt outlined, David managed to fit in a few stops of his own—like Belgian Gelato. After Whitt stopped at two of her favorite galleries, David was ready for dessert and the gelateria was on the way. The two sat in the nearby park, licking ice cream–filled waffle cones and watching the water.

"I kind of like this town. It has a laid-back vibe that I hadn't imagined. I don't know what I thought. Maybe something more buttoned-up and straightlaced."

"Well, relatively speaking, Charleston is less wild than its water-side cousins, Savannah and New Orleans, but it has a racy side, too. The nickname 'the Holy City' is somewhat of a misnomer." Whitt snickered. "Mama calls the three cities 'the Three Sisters'—Mad, Bad, and Glad. She says folks from Savannah are just plain crazy or mad. New Orleans is sometimes called the Devil's Daughter, so she says they're bad. And her people from here, Charleston, are just naughty or glad. Mad, Bad, and Glad!"

"Then maybe it's just your mother who's proper and all. To be honest, she scares me!"

"Mama?" Whitt chuckled at the perception but then reconsidered. "I guess she can be scary at times. Especially when she gives you The Look. She can freeze blood!"

Whitt stood and waited for David to pop the last bite of her unfinished cone in his mouth before she finished her thought. "I think you have to differentiate between 'straightlaced,' like the church ladies, and 'polite,' which Mama and most other Southern ladies would consider themselves. They have a code of behavior and manners that might seem old-fashioned, but they are hardly straightlaced. You'll see that for yourself when you get to the house. They can be pretty bawdy when they're behind closed doors!"

"Your mother bawdy? I can't wait to see that!"

"Oh, she and her sisters and cousins are a hoot when they're cooking and talking in the kitchen. That's the inner sanctum. Normally women only. The men in the family are good cooks, but the women clear the kitchen when the men come in to cook. Messes with the female mojo. So we move to the piazza with sweet tea—or wine—and leave the cooking to the guys on those days. You'll see."

"Can't wait," David muttered, with some uncertainty. "Shall we continue on the tour, madam director?"

Some two hours later, they were finally back at the Rutledge house. David lugged the four heavy suitcases and two carry-ons one by one up to the top of the stairs.

"Which room are we in?" he asked, when the last one had been deposited on the landing. Whitt climbed the stairs behind him and stopped in the middle of the plush Tabriz that carpeted the vestibule of that first level.

"Finley said we were to take the master suite, which is on this floor to the left." She was reading the text her sister had sent that covered the room assignments and house rules. "She says it's the robin's-egg blue room."

David left the bags where they were and went in search of the master suite. "I am not moving another thing until I know where the bags are going! Did you bring the insides of both houses with you? These bags are leaden. I'm surprised that we didn't have to pay overage."

"We did, but they allowed us a waiver. As much as we travel, that airline can't afford to piss us off just because of a few pounds!"

Whitt trotted after David and stopped at the threshold of a massive room that was anchored by a stylized ebony four-poster bed at one end and an elegantly upholstered chaise longue at the other. Nestled between the French doors leading out to the piazza was a small sitting area with two linen-covered chairs and a small glass table. An iron-gated fireplace graced the facing wall.

"Wow! This is nice! Really nice!" Whitt squealed. "Let's move the bags in and then see the other rooms before we start to unpack."

Whitt helped David pull the suitcases into their room, and then together they set off to investigate each of the other rooms. There were three more lavishly appointed bedrooms on that floor, each with a bath en suite. On the floor above, they found the suite that Finley and Max had claimed, as well as two more bedrooms with a shared bath. Above that was the widow's walk. Whitt shuddered when she saw the stairs leading to the upper level. Something in the recesses of her memory said that wasn't a place she wanted to go, but she couldn't recall why.

According to Finley's room roster, Kirsten Brandt, Whitt's best friend from graduate school, and her husband, Reid Perez, were to take the first-floor bedroom so that Kirsten, who was six months pregnant with twins, didn't have to navigate the stairs. Logan Reynolds, a former suitor of Finley who was now one of David's business partners, and his girlfriend, Hema Gupta, along with Charlie Larson, Whitt's best friend from Manila and one of her bridesmaids, would join Whitt and David on the second floor. Finley and Max would take the third-floor suite, a funky, loft-like space that sat under the dormer with an open brick wall and palladium window. Mooney Allen, Finley's dearest friend, and her new beau, Ian Bishop, would occupy one of the other rooms on that floor. That left two rooms for Evans to choose from.

"Does this place ever end? You could get lost in here and it would be days before they found you!" David had made it up to the third floor and was throwing open doors to the bedrooms to peek inside. "How many rooms is that—six, seven? Your sister has great taste. We've stayed in some nice places over the years, but this one takes the prize!"

Whitt started back down the stairs. "On that, I have to agree. We can sing her praises when she gets here. But now, let's get unpacked. Mama is going to want to see us as soon as they get here, and I'm going to need a short nap before then. Jetlag is starting to hit."

"Okay. Why don't we start filling the closet in our room with your things first and then fit mine in as we have room? If necessary, I can hang things in the armoire on the landing."

"As you wish, kind sir." Whitt moved toward the closet's double doors while David laid one of her oversized bags on the floor and began to unzip it. Whitt turned to see which of the two suitcases he had opened just as she swung open the closet doors. She smelled it before she saw it—a sour odor that didn't suit the pristine surroundings. As the doors parted, a sleeping bag rolled to the floor and rested in the threshold of the closet, half in and half out. A hand protruded through a small opening at the top, the drawstring of the sleeping bag pulled tightly around it.

"What the hell is that?" David stopped after two strides forward, meeting Whitt as she stepped back.

"From what I can see, it's a body," Whitt whispered, as she slowly rezipped her suitcase. "We need to call the police."

3

WHEN TWO POLICEMEN ARRIVED FIFTEEN minutes later, Whitt and David were sitting on the front porch, waiting. They had left the room as it was when the body fell. Whitt had simply collected her satchel and closed the bedroom door. She had considered pulling her suitcases out into the hall but didn't want to disturb a crime scene. She figured the low-level stench from the body wouldn't permeate the clothes in zipped suitcases in the next twenty to thirty minutes. Hopefully, the police would then let them retrieve the suitcases and head to a hotel until they were finished investigating.

"Hello, I'm Officer Tremaine Cabot of the Charleston Police Department," a stocky young man who looked like he'd been a Roman wrestler in high school introduced himself. He had light-brown hair and intense dark eyes that he narrowed to make himself appear more serious and consequential. He gestured in the direction of a petite woman with café-au-lait skin and a mop of reddish-brown ringlets that escaped into her face when she walked despite the headband she used to try to contain them. "This is my partner, Officer Nora Horton. Someone called about a body?"

David rose from the porch swing. "Yes. In the upstairs master. It just fell out of the closet when we opened it."

"And you are, sir?" Officer Horton inquired, pulling a small spiral pad from her pocket. "You own this property?"

"I'm David Quinn. And no, we don't own it. We're renting it for the next several weeks. We just arrived today."

"So, you arrived today and found a body upstairs. What time did you arrive, sir?" Officer Horton continued.

"We got in around eleven or so from Atlanta," David responded.

"But it's after 4:00 p.m., sir. You were with the body that whole time?"

"No! We just discovered the body a few minutes ago and called you immediately. We dropped our bags downstairs when we got here and went to grab breakfast," David relayed.

"Then we decided to walk off brunch and do a bit of sightseeing. We had no idea what was in the room!" Whitt declared.

"Okay, so you came from Atlanta this morning by car?"

"No, by plane. We rented the car at the airport."

"So, you flew from Atlanta, where you live, to Charleston, for a few weeks' vacation in a mansion?" Officer Horton arched an eyebrow as if to suggest there was something she wasn't fully understanding.

"I don't live in Atlanta," David explained. "I live in Georgia."

The two police officers looked at each other and then back at David. "Sir, Atlanta is in Georgia," Officer Cabot interjected.

"Not that Georgia, the other one—" David started to clarify, but Whitt interrupted.

"I think there is a misunderstanding here. My fiancé lives in Georgia, the country—in Tbilisi. We flew in from Doha yesterday and spent the night in Atlanta before coming here, to Charleston, on the morning flight. We then rented a car at the Charleston airport and drove here, arriving at about eleven."

"A few more questions, ma'am, before you show us the body," Officer Cabot jumped in. "Who are you, ma'am, and are you also from Georgia, the other Georgia?"

"No, I live in Manila, in the Philippines. My name is Whitt Blake, and we came here for my—our—wedding. We rented the house for the wedding party while they're here. My sister and her partner will be coming in a couple of hours."

Whitt paused and looked up at David, panic flooding her face. "Good Lord! David, we have Finley and Max coming and nowhere to stay. We—they—can't stay *here*. That would just be beyond the pale. And then we have all the other people coming in over the next few days. What are we going to do with them? David, this is a disaster!"

David went over to Whitt and placed his arm around her shoulder. "Let's focus on answering the officers' questions, and then we'll deal with Finley and Max and where we're going to stay. We can call your folks and, if worse comes to worst, we can camp on the couch at their house, okay?" He smiled to reassure her. "It'll be okay."

"Sir, you have family in the area?" Officer Horton queried.

Whitt recovered enough to answer. "I'm actually the one with family in this area. My mother and her family are from Charleston. Sullivan's, actually."

"And the family name is?"

"Montgomery. My grandfather was Harland Montgomery."

After a brief glance at one another, both officers' demeanors changed. "Yes, ma'am. Let's go inside and see what we have."

David opened the door and stood aside to let the officers and Whitt enter. Whitt led the way up the stairs and to the left, toward the master bedroom. At the closed bedroom door, she took a deep breath, preparing for a wave of putrid air. But, besides a little sourness, like when milk has gone bad in the fridge, there was no rancid smell when they entered. There was no need to point out the body. It was there, in full view. The gray sleeping bag with its bright-orange cord. The extended arm reaching through the small opening, as if begging for help.

Whitt inched back as the two officers approached the prone figure and began snapping pictures with their phones. David joined

Whitt in front of the fireplace and watched the officers survey the site. In short time, two more officers arrived. They walked around the cocoonlike shape, and one began taking more formal shots, before Officer Cabot bent down to untie the cord and pull back the nylon covering. The cause of death was apparent. A large dent in the man's right temple was now encrusted with brown and maroon flecks. The flash of the camera made the severity of the wound more graphic with each flare of bright light.

As the rest of the man's features became visible, Whitt drew in a breath and held it as horror twisted her visage. Officer Horton, who had been standing near the closet doors, stared at Whitt with an unwavering gaze.

"Do you know this person?" Horton inquired, her voice hard.

"I don't know him, but I recognize his face from somewhere. I can't place where, though."

The officers had peeled back the sleeping bag to reveal a man of medium height and build with few distinguishing features except his beard—and the gash in his head.

"Was it somewhere recently? Or in the past? Can you be more specific?" Horton probed further, her tone now purposefully neutral.

"I can't say. I can't remember. He just looks vaguely familiar." Whitt continued to stare down at the man. "I wish I could recall more, but all I see is a flash of that face."

"Perhaps you can describe the surroundings? Were there other people? Were you alone? Indoors? Outside?" The officer offered carefully paced prompts to help trigger Whitt's memory.

Whitt shook her head. "So sorry. All I can see is his face. There may have been other people. And I think we made eye contact, but I don't know. It's all muddled."

"Can you narrow down when this occurred? Last year, last week, yesterday? Anything." Horton's voice remained modulated, but her frustration was clear. She glanced at her partner, who looked up from examining the body. She nodded slightly and returned her gaze to Whitt.

Whitt met Horton's gaze. "Well, it wasn't last year because I haven't been home to Charleston in over two years, and it wasn't last week because I was in Mumbai until the day before yesterday. If it was yesterday, it was in the Atlanta airport, since there and the St. Regis are the only places I've been since I left Doha. So, you tell me, because your guess is as good as mine!"

David touched her arm gently and kissed her forehead. "Whitt, honey, it'll be okay. It'll come back to you if it matters. It could have been someone in the airport who looked like him. You're jetlagged, too, so take it easy."

Horton nodded at David and then turned to concentrate her attention on Cabot. They conferred for a few minutes before Horton stuck her head back into the recesses of the closet and Cabot started a walk around the master bedroom. After a time, he pulled out his phone and began a conversation in a muted voice.

David lowered his head to meet Whitt's. She was leaning back against the mantel, staring at the man on the floor, who was dressed in what appeared to have been a neatly pressed pair of khaki trousers and a blue-and-white striped button-down shirt when he'd started the day of his death, whenever that was. Her brow furrowed in concentration. Who was he? And why did he look so familiar?

David whispered in her ear, "It will come. Don't try so hard." He pulled her close and kissed her hair. "Hey, what was with the change in these guys when you mentioned your grandfather's name? It was like you mentioned Gandhi."

Whitt smiled. "Not quite. But my grandaddy was known in these parts. He was a successful businessman who contributed a lot to causes—and people—in Charleston and on Sullivan's. Whites and Blacks both respected him. And everyone knew Granny. She wasn't one to stay under the radar. So, the Montgomery name is known."

"Good to know! I will try not to tarnish the family name." David chuckled at the thought that he was marrying into a branch of the royal family of Charleston.

"Ms. Blake, Mr. Quinn, we have a few more hours of investigating to do." Cabot looked around as he spoke. "This is a big house, and we need to go over every inch of it to see what we can find. I'm going to suggest that you call someone to take you to Sullivan's or a hotel for the next few days. We will let you know when we're done."

"Next few days?" Whitt's eyed widened into saucers. "We're getting married in the next few days! Are you saying that we won't be able to get into the house until after the wedding?"

"Ma'am, we'll work as fast as we can, but this is a murder investigation, and we don't want to overlook anything. If you can answer a couple more questions and then allow the officers to take a look inside your suitcases, we'll let you go to your family. We will ask that you don't leave the area—which we know is unlikely since you're getting married—and leave an address and number where we can reach you."

While David unzipped the suitcases and allowed one of the junior officers to rummage through Whitt's underwear, David's clean shirts, and an array of gifts from India, the Philippines, and Georgia that they had brought for friends and family, Whitt called her daddy and tried to explain what had happened, between interruptions from Mama. Upon hearing the word "body," Mama snatched the phone from her husband and began her own interrogation. Daddy agreed to come over and wait with them until Finley and Max arrived in another hour or so.

When Daddy drove up almost an hour later, Whitt and David had moved themselves into the sun porch and were sipping a glass of the champagne that the house manager, none other than Whitt's cousin Lael, had left for them with a note about having a pleasant stay and an "auspicious beginning to their new life together."

Whitt had broken into fits of stifled laughter when she read the last line. She glanced guiltily around her, aware that the police were probably listening to their every word, convinced that they had somehow offed the poor man upstairs and craftily hidden their heinous crime.

"That is *so* rich! I hope this bears no resemblance to the future that we'll have together," Whitt muttered, as she put down the note and picked up her champagne. "If I didn't know better, I would swear Lael planned this on purpose!"

"Whitt, you can't mean that. I know you said you don't like her, but your cousin had nothing to do with this," David admonished. "Don't you think you had better call her and let her know what's going on?"

Whitt took a long swig of her champagne. "I will leave it to Finley to handle. She made the housing arrangements. Besides, she's better at these things than I am. Just my luck, Lael will say something, and I'll fly off and disinvite her from the wedding. Won't Mama love that!"

A few minutes later, Daddy, a physically imposing man with a gentle heart, arrived. He only half knocked at the door when he came in, his focus on Whitt, whom he enveloped in a bear hug. He continued kissing his daughter's head while he reached over and shook David's hand.

"You want to tell me what's going on while we wait for Finley? She called and said they'd landed. I didn't want to worry her, so I just told her I would meet them here. I'm sure she could hear all the chatter in the background, but there wasn't a thing she could do, and you two are safe. Thank goodness." He gave Whitt another peck on her head. "Do they think it's a robbery gone bad? But that doesn't make sense. What are the cops saying?"

"Nothing at this stage. They're going over every inch of the house, taking prints in places. But they don't have any real idea," David related.

"Fill me in. How did you find the body? Was it in the middle of the room or what?" Daddy had moved Whitt to the couch beside David and watched as she took another sip of her champagne.

"Want some?" Whitt held up the bottle to Daddy. He shook his head. "Lael is good for something!"

"Whittaker, be nice! She didn't cause this." Daddy gave a half-hearted imitation of Mama's Look, his green eyes narrowing, his lips drawn tight. His change in countenance, however, had little effect on Whitt's disposition. "So, what happened?"

"We came in from Atlanta, dropped our bags, and then went to get breakfast at Millers. After, we decided to walk around the Battery," Whitt recounted. "And then we headed home to unpack before Finley and Max got here. I went to open the closet to put some stuff in and out popped a sleeping bag stuffed with a body!"

"How did you know it was a body?" Daddy seemed puzzled.

"The arm sticking through the top was a dead giveaway, sir. No pun intended," David stated wryly.

"Good gracious!" Daddy cried. "So sorry you had to go through this, kitten. Once your sister gets here, we'll head back to the house and get you all resettled. Your mama has everything under control, so don't you worry about this disrupting your wedding. We'll take care of everything."

Whitt had no doubt that Daddy and Mama would make every effort to compensate for the "glitch" thrown into the wedding plans, but she also had no doubt that, years down the road, when she and David thought back over the days leading up to their wedding, this was the event that would first come to mind.

"I know, Daddy. It'll be all right. All that matters is that David and I get married." Whitt squeezed David's hand for reassurance and got a peck on the lips for insurance.

"How was your flight into Atlanta?" Daddy asked, directing his question more at David than Whitt. "You had business there?"

"Yes, sir, we're trying to find outlets for some of the Central Asian wines we have access to. There's a guy in Atlanta who has a restaurant group that launched a set of high-end Middle Eastern and Caucasus restaurants in the South and Mid-Atlantic. He indicated an interest, so we took advantage of the layover."

"Sounds promising."

"We hope so, sir. It would allow us to get back to the States more often—and on someone else's dime!" David chuckled.

"What time do you think Finley will get here?" Whitt glanced at her watch. "We had probably better warn her about the police cars. There are a couple out there, and she might get panicked at the sight of them."

"Too late," David mumbled, looking over Daddy's shoulder at the door. At that angle, he had a clear view of Finley jumping out of the car before Max had fully stopped it, bolting up the stairs two at a time, and flinging open the door. In response, before Daddy or Whitt had seen her, David had risen from the couch and met her at the door. "It's all right. Everyone is okay!"

Finley stared at David for ten seconds before stepping around him and launching a torrent of questions at her daddy and sister. "Where's Mama? Who's hurt?" She turned to glare at David. "If everything's okay, then why are all those police cars outside?"

The last question and the angry look came just as Max walked in the door. He gave David a sympathetic smile and shook his hand while waiting for the answer. He too was curious about the police cars.

"Girl, calm down. Everyone—except the body that Whitt and David found upstairs when they arrived—is fine." Daddy came to give Finley a hug and kiss. She exhaled into the comfort of his arms. "Your mama is at the house making preparations for you all to come stay with us until this is all over."

"A body?" Finley lifted her head from her daddy's chest. "Who is it? And why were they *here*? If it were anything else—a snake in the washing machine, an alligator in the bathtub—I would have sworn it was Lael's doing. But a body? That's a little much, even for her."

Whitt lobbed a side comment at Daddy about not being the only one who suspected Lael before she responded to her sister. "The police haven't made an identification yet. They're giving the house a once-over and will for a while, so we have been displaced," Whitt shared. "Mama is expecting us at the house."

Finley sighed and shook her head. "After all that planning to avoid the chaos at the house, we end up with it all the same. Oh, well. It'll all work out, baby sis, it'll all work out." She leaned over and gave her sister a kiss before heading toward the door, where Max and David were still standing. She approached David. "Sorry for being so snarky. Welcome to the family! A family that seems to love a crisis!"

4

Every Light in the House was on when the two cars pulled up to the Sullivan's Island property shortly before eight o'clock that evening. Whitt and David had hopped in the car with Daddy, so they didn't have to give up their prime parking space directly in front of the Rutledge house. Finley and Max followed along in their rental car.

The police were still working, inspecting every surface for prints, checking every cushion and corner for something that the killer had left behind. Officer Cabot anticipated that the investigation would continue well into the night and over the next couple of days. He assured them that they would work as quickly—and as thoroughly—as they could but offered no promises as to when the homicide team would wrap up.

"You'd best just grab your bags and head to the house. Your mama has arranged for you to stay at the Davises' place until all this is over. It can accommodate the whole crew of you." Daddy gave Whitt a side-glance. "And it will keep you away from the chaos. And I assure you, it is indeed chaotic."

"What's Mama doing so much? The rehearsal dinner and the reception itself are catered, so what is she working on?" Whitt asked Daddy on the way over to Sullivan's.

"Darling, don't ask me. There were people in the kitchen baking, others outside barbequing, and then another crew at the dining room table assembling stuff." Daddy laughed. "I just stayed out of the way. And I'd advise you to do the same!"

As she walked in, Whitt realized that Daddy had underplayed the pandemonium in the house. Every room had something going on. If there wasn't a team of cousins cooking or baking, there was a group of family watching TV, playing a game of cards, or talking. Whitt looked over at Finley and shook her head.

"Weddings and funerals. It happens every time," Finley confirmed.

Max and David stood slack-jawed at the hive of activity. Coming from small families, neither had encountered the noise and frenzy that seemed to be taken in stride by Finley and Whitt, who had pushed through the throng of people, mainly women, working the assembly line in the dining room and had darted through a set of swinging doors into another room. Afraid of being left to fend for themselves in unknown territory, the two men nodded and smiled their way toward what appeared to be the kitchen.

The quiet on the other side of the doors was deafening. Max remembered Finley talking about the kitchen as the inner sanctum, the place where the women of the house, their degrees and pedigree notwithstanding, worked in almost silent harmony. He and David watched as Mama and two other women of similar age and stature moved as if in a choreographed dance about the kitchen, from the stove where Mama stood stirring something in a pot, to the counter where another woman with short cropped hair was manning the standing mixer, to the marble center island, where the third woman sat chopping nuts. Beside the last woman sat a mushroom of a woman whose bottom enveloped the stool on which she sat, in sharp contrast to the lithe woman beside her.

"Max, David. Come over here and give me some sugar," Mama crooned. "I can't stop stirring this custard or it'll curdle."

Whitt and Finley giggled as the two men, after a moment's confusion, did as they were told and went to greet Mama with a hug and a kiss on the cheek, like obedient subjects honoring their queen. Her greeting out of the way, Mama turned to the others in the room and began the introductions.

Nodding at the woman at the counter before turning to those at the island, Mama declared, "This is my sister, Peggy. And that's my other sister, Julie, and our cousin, Odessa. Go give them some sugar, too, before they feel slighted."

Again, the two men made the rounds, kissing the other women, who only briefly looked up from their work to acknowledge them.

"Goodness, you boys smell good enough to eat!" Odessa exclaimed after receiving her kisses. She threw a side-glance at Finley and Whitt and smirked. "They're both keepers! You boys got any older brothers?"

David responded shyly, "No, ma'am. Just a younger sister. And Max here is an only child."

"Shame," Odessa drawled. "Damn shame."

"Don't let Odessa rattle you, boys!" Mama laughed before turning to her daughters. "I just wanted to see you briefly. You had better slip out the side door and have your daddy meet you out front. No need to tackle the introductions in the other room tonight. You'll be here until morning!"

Mama went on. "Aunt Cora is waiting for you all over at their place. I sent dinner over since I figured you hadn't eaten, not with all the police craziness."

"Yeah, what happened over at that rental house? A murder?" Odessa chirped, her eyes hungry for some juicy gossip.

"Odessa, we aren't getting into that tonight," Mama warned. "You can quiz them in the morning. They are tired and jetlagged and need rest. And I don't want my quiet disturbed with the sordid details of a murder. Understood?"

Odessa knew when she was beaten and used her silence as assent. Julie elbowed her and whispered, "Told ya you weren't going to get any news tonight!"

Finley took her cue and grabbed Max's hand to lead him through the departure ritual of kisses and goodnights. She remembered when she was little how saying goodbye could take an hour or more. She always remembered to go to the bathroom when she heard her mama say it was time to go. If you didn't need to go before the family started taking their leave, you were sure to need to by the time it was finished. And at that point, Mama wasn't about to wait for any dallying.

When the foursome had slipped out the side door into the yard, Finley paused to send her daddy a text. No sooner had the door closed than a mass of golden fur came bounding around the house and almost knocked her over.

"And who is this?" David was already making friends with the overgrown puppy, who jumped and yipped in excitement.

"This is Daisy Duke! I'm glad Mama reminded me about her as we were leaving," Whitt exclaimed. "We would have had a devil of a time getting her back in the yard if she escaped the gate."

Finley explained, "She's Daddy's new puppy. Not so new now. She's about seven or eight months old. A Christmas present from Mama and us when they got back from holidays in London last year. When Duke died a few years ago, Daddy seemed so lost, we figured another dog was what he needed, and so we got Daisy."

"Beautiful dog!" Max joined in the petting until they heard a short horn toot and headed to Daddy's waiting car. Max caught up to Finley and slipped his arm around her waist. "Maybe we should get a dog to keep us company—until the babies come." Finley could only look at him in surprise for a second before they were greeted by her daddy and whisked off to the Davises'.

The Davises' house was only a block down the street, well within walking distance, but with the suitcases, the car was easier. Its proximity to Mama and Daddy's house, and its location facing the ocean, made it Mama's choice for the wedding reception. Aunt Cora, Mama's cousin, from which side she couldn't remember, and her best friend since childhood, had offered their house for both the wedding and the reception, but Whitt had wanted to have the wedding at the house, for nostalgia's sake. She had conceded, though, to having the reception on the water.

Both the Davises' house and Mama and Daddy's had a lot of history behind them. Mama's daddy, Harland, had bought the Ion Avenue house in the sixties when the government, which had owned the land, decommissioned Fort Moultrie. The houses on the military installation were going for a song, and Grandpa had the money to buy one but had to ask a Jewish business partner of his to transact the purchase for him. Mr. Rosenthal had bought the house, using Grandpa's money, and then sold it to him in another transaction for one dollar. Mr. Rosenthal repeated the transaction for a couple of other families who moved to Sullivan's at the time. And so, Ms. Charlotte, as some members of family called her, and Mr. Harland had moved from the little house in Beaufort to the big old house on Sullivan's.

Shortly after Daddy retired, he and Mama had bought the family house from Granny. It was Grandpa's death two years before and Mama's concern about being so far from her mother as a military wife that had prompted Daddy to put aside his quest for another star and retire from the Army. Granny, a spitfire of a Southern woman, had wielded her power in drawing her daughters near, and, after a particularly contentious period in which the sisters had joined their mother in guilting Mama about a holiday in St. Lucia, Daddy had phoned Ms. Charlotte and promised that he would do his best to be sure that Mama spent more time home with her.

Mama and Daddy had, at first, looked at buying a place in Charleston, but after further thought, decided that buying Granny's house, putting it in trust for the family, and getting a life estate for Mama and Daddy to live there part of the year was the best arrangement. So began the cycle that Mama and Daddy followed for as long as the sisters could remember, both during and after Granny's lifetime, of summers and holidays, from Thanksgiving to Epiphany, at the Sullivan's Island house.

Aunt Cora, a stylish woman of medium height with honeyed skin and inviting brown eyes, greeted them at the door.

"Ry! Girls! It's so good to see you! Come on in," she gushed, taking Finley's and Whitt's hands and drawing them into the foyer. "And which one is the groom?"

Whitt reached out to David. "This is David, my fiancé. Aunt Cora, thanks so much for putting us up. Of all things—a murder! And right before the wedding!"

"Don't you fret, dear. That's what family and friends are for, and your mama and I have been best friends since we set eyes on each other." Aunt Cora turned to Max. "And Finley, who is this handsome gentleman?"

Finley sidled up to Max and made the introduction. Pleasantries concluded, Max and David quickly headed to the cars to help Daddy with the bags, while Aunt Cora led Finley and Whitt into the kitchen.

"We're leaving the house to you. Your Uncle John and I are in the pool house out back. We've had our supper, but your mama was concerned that you hadn't eaten. I left what she brought over for you in the fridge. You know your way around this house so make yourselves at home. Choose whichever rooms you want upstairs, and we'll see you in the morning."

She leaned over and gave each sister a kiss. "There are bottles of white in the wine fridge so help yourselves, and you know where the wine cellar is if you want red. Tell the boys good night for me. Ring if you need anything. So glad you're home."

After Aunt Cora left, Whitt went over and stuck her head in the refrigerator. "Good Lord, Mama must have thought she was feeding an army. Does she think we're going to be hunkered down here for weeks? Come look at this!"

Finley gazed at the Tupperware bowls of green beans, salad, and macaroni and cheese that filled the refrigerator. She peeked inside a few of the stacked aluminum foil packages and found baked Cornish hens and thick slices of honey ham. "I think she just knows her future son-in-law! David will have worked through this by dinnertime tomorrow."

Whitt chuckled. "You're probably right. Speak of the devil!"

"Which devil are you referring to?" Max asked as he came through the door. He kissed Finley gently on the forehead. "Your father said good night and that he'll see you in the morning."

When morning came, the Four Musketeers, as they had taken to calling themselves, were refreshed and refueled early. Finley and Max were up first and made coffee, which they were enjoying on the deck overlooking the infinity pool and the ocean beyond, when Whitt and David came down. The sea was calm except for the line of breakers that repeatedly amassed before crashing on the shore. The foursome sat silently, sipping their coffee and watching the rhythms of the water before getting dressed and walking over to Mama and Daddy's house.

Whatever zen the morning meditation by the ocean had given them was lost as soon as they walked into the house. Many of the people who had populated the dining room, living room, den, and kitchen the evening before were in their same positions, just with different clothes. The noise level had abated somewhat, but the scurrying continued.

"Do you have any idea who all these people are and what they're doing?" Whitt whispered to Finley.

"I remember some of them, but Mama is going to have to help us make the rounds," her sister replied. "As to what they're doing, that's for Mama to say."

At that moment, Mama came through the swinging door from the kitchen. "I thought I heard someone familiar. Janette, please be sure the bows are centered on each one. Thank you, dear."

The young woman smiled meekly and rearranged the bows on several of the chiffon pouches on the table in front of her.

"Mama, what are these?" Whitt held up a sheer, blush-colored sachet.

Mama gently removed the packet from her hand and returned it to its place on the table. "You're going to throw off her count! They are packets of birdseed for throwing after the wedding. What did you think they were?"

Whitt shrugged and headed into the safety of the kitchen. "I hadn't the slightest idea," she muttered.

In the kitchen, things were in full swing. Four cake plates were topped with what appeared to be two pound cakes, a caramel cake, and a coconut cloud. Aunt Julie had switched places with her sister and was now at the mixer, beating what looked to be icing for an Italian Cream cake, while Aunt Peggy was at the island, supervising Odessa in rolling out biscuits, presumably for dinner. Another woman, who Finley guessed was a cousin on her mother's side, given the woman's height and thin body, was sitting at the table that looked out into the landscaped yard, shelling peas into an oversized cooking pot. Their cousin Lael was sitting nearby, nursing a cup of coffee and making patterns with the shriveled, discarded pods.

"Goodness gracious, child. I haven't seen you in forever." The woman stood and gathered Whitt into a tight embrace. "Almost a married woman, eh? Another week or so and the deed will be done!"

The expression on Whitt's face indicated that she hadn't even a faint notion of who the woman was or how they were related. On that score, Finley couldn't help her. Thankfully, Mama saved the day.

"Shug, that child doesn't remember you. She was thirteen when you were last home. That was some fifteen years ago!" Mama scolded. She addressed Whitt. "Baby, this is your cousin Albertine, Lael's mama. She lives in Chicago—and only makes it home from time to time."

Mama arched an eyebrow at the last few words. "And this is my oldest, Finley. Finley, your cousin Albertine. You remember Lael."

Both girls approached Albertine and then Lael for a perfunctory kiss. Albertine returned to her seat at the table and resumed shelling peas.

"Your mama said you had a body in your house yesterday. Any idea how it got there?" Albertine questioned, without looking up from her shelling duties.

Before Mama could redirect the conversation, Odessa joined in. "You were in the house with it all day long? That can't be good juju. You are going need to sage that place before you go back in." She continued with an explanation of why a cleansing would be necessary if the marriage was to get off on the right footing and how a combination of sage and sea grass was the best antidote to bad spirits.

In response, Mama threw down her dish towel and huffed out of the swinging doors. Whitt's eyes grew wide. After a moment's hesitation, she trotted after her mama, leaving Finley to field the barrage of questions and suggestions that came after.

"Your mama doesn't like talking about death and murders and such. But they happen, don't they?" Odessa put the last of the biscuits on the cookie sheet and stuck them in the oven. She shuffled over and rested herself on one of the stools. "Whoever it is that did it better be scared. These girls have solved murders all over the world. They'll have this thing wrapped up before the wedding, mark my words. Put old Chief Lowell to shame, won't you?"

Finley smiled gamely and waited for a chance to escape. She finally broke away with the help of her Aunt Julie, the soothing sister, who requested in her easy drawl that Finley tell her about her trip to Tanzania. After showing the group some pictures of wildebeest calves, giraffes, and lions that she had on her phone, Finley quietly slipped into the dining room and freedom.

She found Mama taking the bridal couple around to be introduced to everyone in the living room. In the den, Max was at the center of a gaggle of ladies, who opened the circle when she approached.

"Here is your lovely wife now!" Finley almost choked in surprise before her expression changed to one of ambiguous amazement. "Your husband says that you two were only recently married. You didn't want a wedding like your sister? Your mama didn't even send out announcements!"

Max wrapped his arm around her waist and drew her close as he stifled a snicker. He watched her face as it struggled to mask her confusion.

She gave him the evil eye as she carefully worded her reply. "Neither Max nor I like big weddings." Finley hoped her smile looked demure and beatific. *He doesn't like weddings at all, truth be told. What was this man thinking! He's kicked the gossip basket over. Better warn Mama—and Daddy!* "So, a small do in London seemed best."

Finley reached for Max's hand and gently drew him aside, all the while smiling at the group of women. "If you ladies will excuse us for a moment, Mama was looking for us," she fibbed.

Max chortled as they walked away, with Finley in the lead, the pasted-on smile never leaving her face. "We need to warn Mama and Daddy!"

"Of what?" Max was puzzled.

"That you said we were married."

"All I did was call you my wife. Which you are, in my mind. They said we were married."

"But then you said it happened recently when they asked, so you, in essence, confirmed us being married."

"Is there a problem with that?" Max inquired, casting a glance at the women, whose circle had tightened. "Why are they staring at you like that?"

"To see if I'm pregnant."

"What?"

"To see if I'm knocked up!" Finley turned her body sideways so that her flat-stomached profile was clearly visible in the sheath she had thrown on that morning. "In the land of big hair and big weddings that is called the South, the only reason *not* to have a big wedding is if you're preggers."

"That's ridiculous!"

Finley kissed Max's incredulous face. "No, darling, that's the South."

45

5

BY THEIR SECOND MORNING IN Charleston, Max and Finley had slipped easily into the American version of their London routine. They were the first ones up in the house and made the first pot of coffee, laying out the breakfast offerings on the counter for Whitt and David to choose from when they came down. They had made a trip to Callie's in the Charleston City Market the day before and picked up some of her frozen cinnamon biscuits as well as some peach butter. Finley had stuck a few biscuits in the oven before her shower, and now the smell of the piping hot bread pervaded the kitchen.

"If they weren't up before, that aroma will have David here in seconds," Max commented.

As if on cue, David's ginger-blond head rounded the corner. He stood in the doorway with a chuffed grin on his face.

"Something smells beyond good. What are you making?" His eyes zeroed in on the bread basket Finley had just filled.

"Fresh biscuits from Callie's. Not as good as my Granny's but way better than mine would ever be. Get a plate and grab some while they are hot," Finley answered. "And there are more where those came from—the freezer!"

"Let me go tell Whitt, and then I'll be back." David shuffled up the stairs to retrieve Whitt.

"You'd better grab a few before he comes back if you want any of this batch," Finley warned. "I'll put some more in."

Max put a couple of biscuits on a plate before reaching in and grabbing two more. "I have yours. Do you want butter or jam?"

Finley kissed his cheek and filled both of their coffee cups. "Thanks. Just a spot of jam on mine."

On the deck, Finley and Max settled themselves on the chaises that looked out to the water and tucked into their breakfast.

"Anyone want eggs? David's going to make some." Whitt padded out in her bare feet and bent to kiss her sister good morning. "This weather is delightful. I hope it holds."

Max shook his head to the eggs, as did Finley, who asked, "Did you sleep well?"

Whitt hesitated before responding. "Rather fitfully, unfortunately. I hope I didn't keep David awake. There are just so many things running through my mind. The wedding, all the stuff that Mama is adding in, everyone coming in. And then there's the murder. And the fact that the guy looked so familiar."

"Well, you can only control so much. Let Mama do what Mama's going to do—that, you have absolutely no control over, and you need to accept it. The same with the murder. Let the police do their job and contribute where you can," Finley advised. "And with the rest of it, just enjoy the experience. You'll soon have all your friends here to help you celebrate. So, focus on that. Celebrating!"

Whitt leaned down and gave her sister another kiss. "How did you get so wise? Max, you better cherish her. You won't find any better!"

"I know. That's why I like keeping her close," Max mumbled, his mouth filled with warm biscuit, as he reached out to touch Finley's arm.

"I'm going to head back in and help David. Let me know if I can bring you anything. Love you both." Whitt wandered back through the folding glass panels and into the kitchen.

Several minutes later, Whitt came back onto the deck, followed by David, each with a plate of eggs and biscuits and a mug of coffee. "You sure we can't tempt you?" she asked.

"Nope, my biscuits were enough. I gave Max half of my other one. They are good, though! Did you get the other ones out of the oven for me?' Finley looked at her sister, who nodded and pointed at David's plate, onto which five biscuits had been heaped.

"I'm a happy man! So, what's the plan for today?" David asked between bites of buttered biscuit and jam. "Thanks for these, by the way. They are something else. We're going to have to go and restock if anybody else wants any!"

Finley laughed at her soon-to-be brother-in-law. *That boy can eat. I wonder what he's going to look like at fifty. Probably just as trim. Some people just got it in their genes.*

"We have final dress fittings this afternoon." Finley ran through the checklist. "Whitt said Kirsten will be bringing all today's arrivals from the airport this morning around ten. I figured we could head downtown for brunch to keep them occupied and out of Mama's hair. And then we can drop them back here before we grab Charlie and Mama for the bridal shop."

Finley stood and reached for Max's plate. "Right now, I'm going to get Daisy and take her for a long walk. It's early, so I should be able to let her off leash on the beach. Daddy says she's been neglected while he's been running errands for Mama."

"I'll go with you." Max rose from the chaise.

"Swing by here on your way to the beach. By that time, we'll have finished eating and gotten dressed," Whitt urged. Knowing her tendency to take forever to get ready, she added, "And I promise not to slow you down!"

True to her word, Whitt and David were waiting at the end of the Davises' driveway when Max and Finley came by with an ebullient Daisy. The puppy wanted to break form and rush to greet David, but she knew better and responded to Finley's subtle commands. Daddy had trained her well. As Finley drew alongside David, she commanded Daisy to sit and wait before releasing her. Finley had barely completed the okay command before Daisy ran into David's arms.

"I think somebody's in love!" Finley teased. "Whitt, you'd better reconsider this wedding. David's playing around with another girl."

David wrapped his arms around Whitt and closed the space between them. "I love you, Daisy, but no one gets between me and this woman."

Daisy eyed David and then Whitt before trotting back to sit at Finley's feet. "Fickle girl," Finley remarked. She headed down the street with Daisy heeling right beside her. "Let's head along the beach to the lighthouse. She can get a little time off leash."

At the beach, Daisy acted like the puppy she was, dancing in the waves as they lapped the sand and running like the devil was chasing her along the wide expanse of shore. Max and Finley had set a fast pace to ensure the retriever was always in sight, while David and Whitt strolled along behind, arm in arm. Periodically, Finley would clap her hands or whistle to call Daisy back to her side.

"She's really well trained," Max observed as they walked along.

"Daddy wouldn't have it any other way. He takes pride in his dogs and their training. Nothing upsets him more than a spoiled, undisciplined hound." Finley giggled at her daddy's reaction to dogs that jumped on people or had bad cases of what he called the zoomies—those times when energy compels a dog to spin in circles, chasing its tail. "Give him a little time and this one will be handled with just hand signals and whistles. That's a sight to see."

"Whitt seems upset about not being able to remember the man they found dead in the house," Max noticed. "Is it just bugging her that she can't remember or is she afraid that someone is after her?"

Finley stopped. She looked back at her sister. "I never asked, but now that you mention it . . . I just assumed it was the former, but given all the troubles we've been in, she may be thinking something in the past is coming to haunt her. When we stop for coffee at the lighthouse, I'll ask."

The walk up the beach to the lighthouse took Finley and Max twenty minutes, but Whitt and David, who stopped from time to time for private conversations and a few secret kisses, needed another ten minutes. While they waited, Max and Finley sat at one of the picnic tables, her head on his shoulder, and watched the waves come in. Daisy, tired from her exuberant jaunt, rested her head on Max's deck shoes and was soon fast asleep.

"You guys ready for more coffee?" David asked when he and Whitt finally arrived. He knew the standing order for each of them, depending on the time of day. This time of morning, Finley and Max would be ready for another cup of black coffee, while Whitt would likely switch to tea. He was ready for something else to eat and a latte. "Anything to eat?"

Finley feigned surprise at the last question and then shook her head. Max asked for a croissant. When Whitt and David returned with their drinks and food, Daisy raised her head, confirmed that the pack was safe, and went back to sleep.

"We haven't done that walk along the beach in a while! Not since Duke died," Whitt noted, glancing at Daisy. "It's nice having a dog again."

Max nudged Finley with his elbow and whispered, "That's what I was saying."

"But your rationale was different, as I recall," Finley retorted under her breath. Whitt and David observed the exchange, simply shrugging when they failed to understand its meaning.

Finley returned her attention to her sister. "Have you thought any more about the murder and who the man might be? If you don't want to talk about it, just say so."

"I don't mind talking about it, but I don't have any more idea now than I did yesterday or the day before." Whitt sighed. "I swear I knew him from somewhere—but where? School? Or work? Or someplace that I've traveled to? I wish you'd been there to see him. If he was from around here, you might have been able to place him."

"Are you just puzzled as to who he is or are you afraid that you can't recognize him?" Finley asked.

"Afraid? Why?" David questioned.

"Well, they've been in some pretty tough spots with some less than savory characters," Max reminded. "We were just wondering. It might also help you figure out where you know him from."

Whitt thought for moment. "No, I'm not scared. I don't think he was anyone from overseas. The more I think about it, the more I'm sure he was someone we know from here— from Charleston."

"How old was he? Was he tall or short? Any distinguishing features?" Finley peppered her sister with questions. She'd entered investigative mode now and was methodically gathering facts that might help her solve the puzzle. Max's cheek dimpled as he listened to her.

Whitt and David took turns detailing the man's description and illustrating his body position and the location of the wound on his head. Finley was glad they were the only ones on the café patio, given the gory nature of their conversation. Despite the detailed recounting of their discovery of the body, Whitt was still unable to identify him.

I wish I'd had a chance to look at the body. I might be able to trigger Whitt's memory. This is starting to get to her, and she doesn't need any distraction before the wedding. The justice of the peace is looking better and better, Finley thought.

By the time they got back to Aunt Cora and Uncle John's house, Finley only had a few minutes to hose the sand off Daisy before a gray minivan pulled up and the airport crew piled out. Finley tied up Daisy and went to greet everyone. She hadn't seen Kirsten, Whitt's best friend from graduate school, in almost five years—since Kirsten had come up to DC for a farewell party for Whitt before she headed off to Manila. It'd been before Finley and Max broke up, while she was on home leave for Whitt's graduation. Little did Finley know that only a few months later, her whole world would be upended and her heart broken, almost irreparably.

"Isn't she just glowing?" Whitt remarked to Finley, as she joined the group after securing Daisy. Whitt's arm was around a curvaceous woman with a rounded, expectant belly. Finley had remembered Kirsten as prematurely gray, but now her hair was a rich, dark brown with red highlights in the sunlight. She did look radiant.

Finley gave her a side hug, getting a kick in the ribs midembrace from a tiny, in utero foot. "Sorry about that. These babies like their space. They guard it with their little feet and can sense people coming at twenty paces!" Kirsten joked. "And that glow Whitt is talking about is just plain old sweat. It's hot as Hades around here. Or is it just me?"

Finley chuckled. She had always liked Kirsten's irreverent—sometimes bawdy—humor. She turned to the tall, dark-haired man who stood some distance away from Kirsten, making polite conversation with a petite, strawberry-blond woman Findley assumed was Charlie Larson, Whitt's best friend and running pal in Manila. "You must be Reid," Finley said to the man, before turning to address the woman. "And you must be Charlie." She hugged each in turn.

She leaned across to Max, who stood near the van, helping to unload suitcases. "Have you met Max?" she inquired. The other two nodded. She gestured toward Logan and Hema. "And I figure you guys introduced yourselves to Logan and Hema during the drive from the airport."

Before she could excuse herself, she was wrapped in a tight, enveloping hug that almost swept her off her feet. It was Logan Reynolds, a very handsome, very wealthy New Yorker whom Mooney had tried to hitch Finley's wagon to, without result.

"How I have missed you! Your moving to London has left me with no one in New York to kvetch with. Cork hasn't been the same since you left." Logan raised the hand of a beautiful woman in an embroidered, blue shalwar kameez. Hema, a sassy radiologist, had caught Logan's eye in Jaipur and had been by his side ever since. "Hema listens, but, as she'll tell you herself, she struggles to grasp the concept of a good kvetch. You understand."

Finley planted a kiss on both of Logan's cheeks, her ticket for a quick release from his clinch. She delivered a similar greeting to Hema, who rolled her eyes at Logan's theatrics.

"How do you put up with this man?" Finley asked, as they stood in the driveway. "Why we are all outside in this heat is beyond me. Let's head in."

Finley summoned Whitt over and reminded her of the room options as the group headed into the house. While Whitt took Kirsten and Reid to their room on the ground floor, Finley gave the others a tour of the rest of the house.

"Don't get too settled," Finley advised, after offering coffee and sweet tea all around. "If you're up for it, we're going to head into town and do a short tour of Charleston to get you oriented. You can do a more extensive walkabout later, on your own, if you'd like."

The group loaded back into the van and Max and Finley's rented SUV, striking out for downtown Charleston. While Kirsten, a native South Carolinian, had been to the city several times, Reid and the others had not. The carriage tour planned for Thursday, when most of the out-of-town guests would be in, would give them more history. Today's trip was primarily designed to distract Whitt until the fitting and keep her out of Mama's hair.

Finley had been tempted to skip the tour and help Mama with her cooking and favor making—more to gather intelligence that would put Whitt's mind at ease than to actually engage in any of the activities. But she thought better of it. She and Whitt were the only two who really knew the city and if Kirsten got tired and Whitt wanted to sit with her, there would be no tour guide. Besides, if she stayed behind, Whitt might get the notion to do the same and the whole reason for the outing in the first place would be shot to hell.

After pulling the cars into a lot off King, the crew made their way to Toast!, a quaint restaurant in the French Quarter known for its stuffed French toast, and waffles and fried chicken. Besides the fact that David was hungry again, the strategy was to get the new arrivals into a food and drink stupor deep enough that they would need a nap or a lie by the pool after the tour so that they wouldn't need to be entertained while the wedding party took Whitt for her last fitting.

A chatty waitress, curious about where this motley crew was coming from, quizzed them the entire way to the mezzanine, where two large rectangular tables had been pushed together to accommodate the large—and noisy—group.

"They're trying to hide us away because we are so loud and boisterous," Kirsten commented. "They should be jumping for joy that I can't drink, or I'd be swinging from the rafters and leading the singalong after a couple of pitchers of their tequila sunrise mimosas."

"Are those good?" Logan inquired, looking around at the drinks on the other tables to see if he could spy what they looked like.

"Don't give Logan any ideas!" Finley teased. "This man will drink us all under the table and be looking for more."

"And I do get animated when that happens." Logan laughed at the startled look in Hema's eyes. "But I promise not to embarrass you."

The crew had barely ordered when Logan asked the question that had been on everyone's mind. "Okay, now tell us about this murder that has displaced us for the next few days! You just opened the door and there it was?"

David deferred to Whitt, who launched into a detailed recitation of their first day in Charleston. She had them in stitches as she described Max and David's reaction to the madness in her parents' house when they'd walked in that first night.

"We walked into the dining room, and it look like Grand Central Station at rush hour, except these ladies were focused on getting the job done. These guys stopped midstep, and their jaws hit the ground." Whitt tittered at the mental image of their faces. "I only learned later that the ladies were stuffing birdseed sachets for throwing after the ceremony! Mama has every little detail down. Why we need them, I will never know."

"But back to the body y'all found in the house." Kirsten took a sip of her sweet tea as she directed the question to Whitt. "Do the police think it was dumped there, or did the killer do the deed right there?"

"Pregnancy hasn't cleansed your sordid mind. Not one bit," Whitt mused. "The cops don't know, or if they do, they aren't talking to us about it."

"It's only been a couple of days. It may take them some time to figure this out," Finley observed.

"Appreciated, but it's just that a murder wasn't exactly what I had envisioned as part of the wedding festivities," Whitt said quietly, a slight catch in her voice.

Finley touched her sister's shoulder gently, as the chatter around the table continued. "No, it's not, but it may be too much for anyone to deliver right now. That you can't control, kid. All you can do is have a good time with whatever happens. And that will be our collective focus—making sure you and David have a great time at your wedding . . . whether the murder is solved or not."

6

ANOTHER FEW SUNRISE MIMOSAS TOOK care of Whitt's momentary funk, and the rest of the morning went as planned. When the crew got back to the Davises' house just after one, another delivery of food had been made and the refrigerator was once again filled to overflowing. As predicted, David had eaten all but a drumstick and a single slice of ham from the food Mama had brought over a day ago. This time, she'd cooked two chickens, another ham, a lasagna, and an array of sides. Her note simply read, *Something to hold you over between meals. Enjoy. Love, Mama.* On the counter, she had also left a container of brownies and a deep-dish apple pie.

"Goodness, who's going to eat all this?" Charlie questioned. "And your mom's note makes it sound like this isn't the meal. Just a snack."

Max snickered. "David—and, as I recall, Logan—will descend on these like a horde of locusts. Mrs. Blake is their savior and they're her favored children. Food is love around here."

Reid nodded. "I come from Texas, and food is love there, too. You know when my mother doesn't like someone. She offers them something to drink. Period. If there's no slice of cake or cookies brought with the cup of coffee or glass of Coke, she wants you gone."

"So that's what she was trying to tell me when we were dating," Kirsten kidded, as she touched her husband's cheek before resting her hand on her stomach. "Sorry, I didn't get the message. Too late now!"

While David and Whitt looked through the foil and ziplocked packages, the rest of the crew broke off to take naps, grab showers, or unpack. Max poured himself and Finley the last of the coffee and stuck it in the microwave to warm while he made another pot. When the coffee was ready, he took three brownies from the tin and headed out to the deck. Finley had already claimed a spot for them on the chaises under the umbrella.

"Brought you one of your mother's brownies before they're all gone." Max placed their coffees on the table between them and opened the napkin that he clutched in his fist to reveal the dark chocolate squares. "If we don't grab them now, we'll be eating crumbs."

"We can always make another batch. Besides, something else will be on the menu tomorrow. Remember Mama and Aunt Julie were making trifle and banana pudding when we picked up Daisy this morning. I might be able to steal some of that for you when I head over to the house later." At the mention of her name, Daisy scampered over from her spot on the grass to lie at Finley's feet. "Then there'll be a cobbler in the mix at some point."

"Thanks. Not that I need any of this." Max stretched his long body out on the chaise and took a slow sip of his coffee. "Nice group of friends Whitt has. It's nice having everybody around." He paused. His gaze was out to sea. "I'm sorry."

Finley turned to look at him, her forehead creased, her eyes searching his face for some indication of a problem. "For what?"

"For making you miss all of this." He inclined his head toward the inside of the house, where Whitt, David, Charlie, and Hema had reassembled. They were talking over each other and laughing about something. "The wedding preparations, the friends coming in, the memories."

His bright-blue eyes clouded with sadness or regret—she couldn't tell which—and fixed on an invisible point on the horizon. Her eyes followed his line of sight. The illusion created by the infinity pool, the ocean, and the sky was one of horizontal ribbons of blue that claimed the visual field from the ground to the horizon and beyond. For a moment, she felt like she was floating, drifting away—away from him, in this flash flood of sadness that he had suddenly unleashed.

To ground herself, Finley swung her legs off the chaise so that she was sitting, feet down, facing him. "Max, you didn't make me miss anything. When we committed, the only person I needed there was you. And you are here now." Her voice was strong, yet gentle and loving. "I sure didn't need this craziness! The only person who wasn't there was Mooney, and she's forgiven me. Was there someone you would've had there?"

Max tilted his head toward her and gave her a sad smile. "No. All I needed there was you. You're all I've ever needed."

"Are you sure? No friends you would've invited? No college roommates?" She smirked. "No old girlfriends? Just for spite!"

"Nope." Max flashed a crooked grin at the last comment, the melancholic moment having passed.

Finley, seeing the change in his mood, hesitated to venture where her next question might take them but pushed forward anyway. She absentmindedly twisted the band on her ring finger. "Max, do your parents know about us?"

Max drew in a deep breath and then exhaled slowly. He opened his mouth to speak but then zipped it, rubbing his thumb back and forth across his bottom lip. The few seconds of contemplation felt like hours to Finley, but she waited. In time, he spoke. "Yes. I've told them about you…about us. I talk about you often. But I don't know that it matters." Max watched her face. He saw her jaw tense and begin the oscillating motion it did when she was distressed.

"What do you mean?" She enunciated every word carefully, her eyes following the line of his jaw and then the curve of his mouth. Again, she waited for him to select the right words. *What did his parents say about me that has him so closemouthed? These people that I've never met, that he has never introduced me to.* Her breath caught in her chest. *Is he ashamed of me?*

"That I've told them about you… from the day I met you. How beautiful you are, how smart. How much in love with you I was—I am." The sad smile returned. "And all either of them ever said was, 'How nice, dear.' Then they would launch into the same diatribe about what the other did to them that I hear every time I call."

He picked the brownie crumbs from his trousers, one at a time. After a time, his hand stilled, and his eyes turned to rest on Finley's face. "What I have been trying to avoid saying is what I have been trying to avoid facing for the longest time. My parents are so wholly self-absorbed that whether we are together or apart doesn't matter to them." Then he chuckled. "Your parents are more interested in my life than my own are! Sad, eh?"

"Max, I'm so sorry. I knew that your relationship with them was complicated, but…"

"You didn't realize it was this hollow?" Max asked. "So, no, there is no one I would have asked to be there if we had gotten married."

"Then we did it the right way. Just us… and eventually Mama, Daddy, Whitt, and David." Finley rose from her chaise and sat down on Max's, facing him. She lifted his hand and kissed his palm, closing his fingers around it. She then placed his fist over his heart. "If ever you forget that someone loves you, you'll have that as proof that someone does."

"Did your mother teach you that?" Max opened his palm and pressed her kiss to his chest.

Finley nodded. "Her love tap. Every first day of school, any time I was scared or sad or disappointed." Her eyes welled up. "By the time I got home from Morocco the first time, my chest was red from tapping it so hard, trying to pour some love back in. And all the while, you could have used a love tap, too."

"Yep." Max caressed her cheek before leaning in to kiss her nose and her forehead. "Thank you for this one." Then he kissed her mouth.

So thorough was his thank-you that Whitt had to clear her throat twice to catch Max and Finley's attention. Even then, Finley took her time pulling away from him, her hand stroking his chest as she looked up to see what Whitt had to say that was so pressing.

"Sorry for interrupting, but Mama said we need to head over to the bridal shop in another half hour. And she wants us to come over now to meet some people who are asking for us." Whitt stood in the patio opening with a smug grin.

"Asking for you!" Finley gave Max another peck on the lips. "I'd better go change and head over to the house. I haven't the slightest idea when the fitting will be over, but we have dinner reservations at the Gin Joint at eight, so you can just hang out here until then."

"We can send Kirsten and the guys over early if we're running late," Whitt recommended. "In the meantime, Reid and Logan are playing pool. I think David's going to take a swim. Or you can nod off right here if you don't want to join in. So many options and so little time!"

When they got to Mama and Daddy's house, they split up. Charlie stayed in the car while Finley took Daisy around to the back. Whitt slipped through the house and into the dining room. The ladies were still assembling, but things were now going into small, handloomed gift bags that were decorated with pressed flowers instead of into yesterday's chiffon sachets. Whitt tried to take a peek into one of the assembled sacks but had it taken from her hand before she could see anything besides tissue paper. "Mrs. Blake said no one but us was to touch these!" she was told by an officious young woman who was probably some cousin or some cousin's friend trying to get in good with Mama.

She went off into the kitchen, grumbling under her breath. *My own damn wedding and I don't know what's going on! Vegas is looking better by the second!* The look her mama gave her when she walked into the kitchen, however, made her change her sour disposition for a sweet, ladylike smile lightning quick.

"There's our bride!" Mama announced, leading Whitt into the room. Fifteen or so women had somehow packed themselves into the large kitchen that could generously fit ten ordinary-sized ladies but was straining under the weight of this group, over half of whom were big-boned girls. "What have you been up to, darling? Your cousins have been waiting to see you!"

Mama started making introductions, and Whitt got into a rhythm of smiling and kissing, without even trying to match names and faces. There were too many, and they all started to sound the same after a while. Even differentiation by dress was complicated; they had all decided to wear some shade of pink or red, from the palest blush, to bubblegum, to brick, to fire-engine.

"Where's your sister?" Mama interrupted the cousins' quizzing of Whitt on the wedding, her travels, and her beau.

"Out back. With Daisy," Whitt responded in between attempts to fill her cousins in on the last ten years of her life.

"Is she dressed? We need to leave in five minutes, and we can't be late." Mama was starting to get exasperated. "Why is your sister doing this to me?"

Finley broke through the group of women crowded near the side door and made herself visible. Her daddy was right behind her. "I'm right here, Mama. Calm down. I had to put Daisy up, and Daddy was introducing me around out back."

Finley waved and made a general introduction that was greeted by a cacophony of voices calling out names. "Nice meeting y'all. I hope you'll excuse us. We have a bride to get fitted."

Finley tried to guide her mama and sister out of the kitchen, but Mama insisted on giving Daddy last-minute instructions. "You and the menfolk have the barbeque taken care of. As soon as it's cut up, let Julie and Peggy know and they will bring out the sides. The table outside already has the plates and utensils out. When you are ready for dessert, just have them bring the cakes out. The ice cream I just churned is in the back freezer. Don't forget to serve it!"

She took a single step. "Oh, and before I forget—Albertine's people from Port Royal made me think of it—we need to head to Beaufort this week to see what the house needs. Ry, sweetie, you've got people working on the roof and don't even know what they're doing," Mama chided. "You trust too much! Let's go Tuesday before David's parents get in. I'll need a break by then!"

Daddy kissed Mama's nose and pushed his wife toward Finley, who had already ushered Whitt through the swinging doors into the dining room. "Whatever you say, darling. Tuesday it is. And we'll get this crowd fed. You just focus on getting fitted!"

Mama kissed her husband and followed her daughters outside to the car. She slid into the front passenger seat while Finley took the wheel. Whitt was grateful for the comforting calm that Charlie, who sat quietly in the back seat, offered. Mama jumped when she caught Charlie's movement in the corner of her eye. "Good gracious, Charlie, you gave me a fright! You're so quiet, child."

Charlie smiled in response and attempted to distract Whitt with a conversation about the bridal shop they were heading to. As her wedding day grew nearer, Whitt alternated between giddy happiness and agitated trepidation. The murder hadn't helped. The police had called with more questions but no answers.

"Have you or Daddy heard from the police? Besides calling with more inane questions, I haven't heard anything," Whitt complained. "I would like to get settled back in the house before the wedding."

Mama shook her head. "And that is the last word I want to hear about it today. We are going to have a good time at the fitting. Just us girls. So, no talk of murder! Understood?"

Finley and Charlie nodded. Whitt harrumphed before muttering a "yes, ma'am."

The bridal salon Whitt had chosen when she and Mama went dress shopping the previous summer was a small boutique not far from the house. Mama would have preferred that Whitt go to one of the larger, exclusive salons in Charleston proper, like Lovely or Maddison Row, to find a bespoke gown, but Whitt had held her ground and insisted on this one.

Whitt had found her dress and those for her two bridesmaids after barely an hour of shopping, much to Mama's dismay. Mama doubted that any self-respecting bride would just grab a dress from the rack without some hemming and hawing. That Whitt had chosen so quickly had Mama on the phone to Finley, wondering how serious Whitt was about having a wedding.

"Have you been talking to your sister, missy?" Mama had inquired when she Facetimed Finley that very afternoon. Mama then recounted the details of the wedding dress shopping expedition and her fear that Whitt was going to cavalierly throw off all the wedding preparations and elope.

"Mama, Whitt and David wouldn't disappoint you and Mrs. Quinn like that. Whitt knows she is your only hope for a wedding, even if it is just a small one!" Finley had crooned, redirecting Mama by quizzing her on the dress's silhouette and the color and shape of the bridesmaid dresses. She knew better than to inquire about the type of veil. Whitt didn't want to wear one—another bone of contention between Whitt and her mama.

The salon was just off the main street in Mt. Pleasant. A compact space, the shop was painted white, with a large picture window that was divided into three panels, each flanked by tall black shutters. In each window hung a suspended hanger on which beaded and chiffoned white dresses were draped. No embellishments. Just the dresses, artfully displayed in the window. As a result, the focus was on the garments.

The minimalist design concept continued inside, where a loft-high ceiling and exposed brick wall dominated the room. Racks of dresses in every hue of white were mounted into industrial tracks along the ceiling, making for easier movement of the voluminous dresses along the rack. White upholstered settees, chairs, and benches were clustered around two tall three-way mirrors, in front of which was a short, raised runway. Crystal vases filled with white calla lilies or roses graced the small pedestal tables dotted around the room. Selections of bridesmaid dresses, the only color in the salon, were closeted in two massive, white-washed armoires along the back wall. The illusion was of a garden of white—white appointments, white flowers, white dresses.

A petite woman with cropped salt-and-pepper hair who was wearing a stylish cream sheath came from behind the counter to greet Mama and Whitt. Were she taller, Finley would have guessed she was another cousin from Mama's side due to the prematurely graying hair. If Mama didn't say, Finley would have to remember to ask later.

"Mrs. Blake and the soon-to-be Mrs. Quinn. How are you?" The woman addressed Whitt. "Excited about the big day? I never asked, but are you going by Quinn or are you keeping your name?"

"I'm keeping my maiden name," Whitt replied. Mama drew back in surprise, seeming a little puzzled. In response, Whitt directed her explanation to Mama. "I had considered taking Quinn, just to make it easy, but then it sounded weird. And then I thought of hyphenating it, but that sounded off, too. So, I'm going to keep the one I was born with."

While Whitt was talking, Mama mouthed the different names and then nodded. "You're right. Your maiden name does sound better."

The woman turned to Finley and Charlie. "I don't believe we've met. I'm Deirdre Ross. And you must be Charlie and Finley. Whitt has mentioned you often." Deirdre turned back to Whitt. "How do you want to work the appointment? We can start with your dress, or we can take care of the bridesmaids first. Which would you prefer?"

Finley could tell from the way Mama sat forward in her seat that she had her preference. But she judiciously held her tongue and left the decision to Whitt.

"Let's do the bridesmaids first. They haven't seen their dresses, and I think their fitting will be pretty quick," Whitt decided.

As it turned out, the entire fitting was quick. Deirdre, whom Finley found out was the owner of the shop, called her seamstress to adjust the straps and hem of Charlie's dress and lengthen Finley's dress an inch. For her bridesmaids, Whitt had chosen a body-skimming silk slip dress in celadon green with a deep vee in both the front and back. As different as the dress looked on Charlie's petite frame and Finley's more statuesque build, the simplicity of the design suited both women's slim figures.

"You look like movie stars from Hollywood in those dresses," Mama cried. "All you need now is a gold cigarette holder and a glass of champagne! Max is going to love that!"

"You like them, Mama? So, they don't look like flophouse floozies?" Whitt stage-whispered into her mama's ear, emphasizing her final words with air quotes.

Mama shooed her daughter away. "I never said that! Now, go try your dress on!"

"Not before you get fitted for yours!" Whitt countered. "Go. Now!"

When Mama returned in her mother-of-the-bride dress—a flowing, blush-colored, V-neck, A-line gown that skimmed the contours of her body with elegant lightweight silk jersey—Whitt was in the showroom, pulling out sample dresses and putting them aside. Finley just shrugged when Mama asked her what Whitt was doing. She instead commented on how regal her mama looked. Deirdre simply smiled and instructed the seamstress to make a few minor adjustments to Mama's dress before sending her into the dressing room to change.

At long last, Deirdre ushered Whitt into a dressing room to change and brought her out some minutes later in her dress for her entourage to see. The dress, a simply structured, strapless white sheath with a slightly trumpeted hemline and chapel train, had a sheer, embroidered shoulder wrap that gave the dress both texture and character. *That dress is so Whitt. Perfectly constructed. Nice clean lines, no fluff or frills. Straight to the point. Perfect*, Finley thought.

"You look so beautiful, baby sis," Finley managed to whisper after a few minutes. "Just ethereally beautiful. Stunning!" she gushed.

Whitt mounted the platform and took in her image in the mirror. She stared, expressionless, for a minute or so.

"Don't you like it? Are you thinking you want something else?" Mama gasped, remembering the other dresses Whitt had set aside. "Whitt, say something!"

Whitt looked at her mother and the others as if awakened from a dream. She stared at their reflections in the mirror wordlessly. Deirdre stood frozen in place, waiting for Whitt's reaction, her face slowly losing color even as she maintained her placid demeanor. Whitt returned her gaze to her reflection in the mirror. A shy smile soon became a jubilant grin and then a satisfied laugh. "I love it. I'm getting married!"

The alterations for Whitt took even less time than those for Charlie and Finley. While Mama talked to Deirdre about when the dresses would be delivered to the house, Whitt pulled Finley over to a station on which several wedding dresses had been placed. Charlie looked through them and then back at Whitt. "Are you getting like Kim Kardashian and making a couple of changes during your wedding?"

"Goodness no! These are for Finley to try," Whitt declared.

Finley whipped around and stared at her sister. "Whatever would I want to do that for? I'm not getting married. Max and I are as married as we're ever going to be."

"Then it won't hurt you to try a few on! We're never going to get to do this, so let's just pretend." Whitt pleaded, "Please!"

"Please what?" Mama asked, as she rejoined the sisters and Charlie.

"Try on a few wedding dresses. Deirdre won't mind," Whitt continued. "You would make such a pretty bride."

Finley shook her head. "We'll do it another time."

"When? We're almost never together. So, humor me. Please!" Whitt grabbed her sister's hand and squeezed it tight. Finley was reminded of the little sister who would cajole her into extra cookies or another half hour of television when Finley babysat. The little sister who could convince her to ask her parents for whatever Whitt wanted because "she was only a kid." She studied Whitt's imploring eyes, her plaintive mouth, and started to giggle.

"You have done it again!" Finley exclaimed. "Give me the dresses so we can get out of here. I know I will find no peace until I try the darn things on, so let's get it over with. As long as Deirdre doesn't mind!"

Deirdre indicated her approval by leading Finley to a dressing room. Charlie expressed an emphatic no to Finley's suggestion that she join her. *I have to give it to Whitt. She knows my style.* Finley looked at the three dresses Whitt had selected, all different shapes but all reflective of Finley's personality—a boatneck silk sheath, a strapless lace trumpet, and a high-necked cap-sleeve A-line.

Finley had almost finished modeling the dresses. Each had been met with sighs and words of approval from her viewing audience. Her favorite had been the first one, the boatneck sheath. She had just stepped onto the pedestal in the cap sleeve A-line and turned to the group when Whitt jumped up, her hand to her mouth. Mama thought she had suddenly remembered someone important who she'd forgotten to invite or a detail in the wedding plans that had been overlooked.

"I know now! Now I remember!" Whitt exclaimed, mounting the platform and taking Finley by the shoulders. "I know where I saw him before! He was at the airport, in line in front of us, when we went to change our flight. He looked at me like he knew me when he turned around. Now I remember!"

7

WHEN THEY WERE ALL BACK in the car, Whitt explained the trigger for her recollection. "It was that last dress Finley tried on. The high neck reminded me of the dress a woman who came up to the airline customer service counter had on. I liked the cut and remarked to David about it right before the man who we found in the rental house turned around and stared at me. The guy looked like he was getting ready to say something, but then we were called to the desk and the moment passed."

"So, you know who he is?" Charlie asked.

"No. That's the thing. I recognize his face, but I don't know him. At least, as far as I can remember," Whitt responded. "But the weird thing is that I have a feeling that wasn't the first time I'd seen him."

Mama turned in the front seat to look at her daughter. "What does that mean? You don't know him, but you 'know' him. From where?"

Whitt shrugged. "Beats me! On that front, I'm as clueless as I was before."

"Not really. You know where you saw him most recently, and you think that you might have met him before. So, that is something to work with. We just need to help trigger your memory about the places you might know him from." Finley started organizing their investigation into the man's identity. "Since we're in Charleston, let's start there."

Before she could offer Whitt some prompts, Mama cut her off, her face flushed. "Girls, I will not have you playing amateur detectives in my presence! I said no murder talk, and I mean it. When you get back to the house, Whittaker, you may call the detective and tell him where you last saw the man. After that, not another word. Is that understood?"

Charlie watched, wide-eyed, as both sisters nodded and murmured their "yes, ma'ams." For the rest of the ride, the car was church quiet. When Mama got out, she waited for Whitt. Finley chortled. Evidently, Mama was planning on supervising Whitt's call to Cabot so there was indeed no further conversation about murder beyond what Mama had sanctioned. She would probably usher Whitt into the back bedroom or her own room and use the phone in there.

"Please wait in the car, ladies!" Mama directed, and Finley and Charlie complied. "We won't be long. I know you have dinner reservations, so I won't keep you," she called back over her shoulder, as she walked briskly into the house.

"Is your mother angry?" Charlie's soft voice came from the back seat.

"No. She just hates it when we play the Murder Game or try to get involved in things that really don't concern us—like murders!" Finley leaned around the seat to look at Charlie. "She gets that tone to her voice, but she knows most of the time we aren't going to listen. You'd have thought she would've given up by now!"

Within minutes, Whitt was back. She slid quickly into the shotgun seat left vacant by Mama. "Let's go. Cabot said he will meet us at the Davises' early tomorrow. Now, I'm ready for a drink."

"Mama okay?" Finley gave her sister a side-glance before starting the car and heading the one block to the Davises' house.

"Yeah. She changed clothes while I called the police and then went into the kitchen." Whitt smiled. "Feeding the masses gets her into her groove. Daddy said everyone had been fed, so she was happy."

The rest of the crew was dressed for dinner and congregating in the kitchen when Finley, Whitt, and Charlie walked into the house. "Here comes the bride!" Kirsten called out when Whitt entered.

David greeted her with a kiss, which prompted a round of glass tapping, demanding that he kiss her again. "This isn't even the dress rehearsal, much less the wedding. I'll respond to the glass taps then." That didn't stop him from giving Whitt another long, smoldering embrace that drew a boisterous response from the crowd.

"David, let her loose so she can go get changed for dinner. You can finish smooching later!" Finley teased. She gave Max a quick peck and headed up the stairs to get changed herself.

She was struggling to zip her dress, almost conceding that she would have to go downstairs to ask someone to help her, when Max slipped behind her and completed the task, giving her neck an extra caress in the process. She turned and rewarded him with a thorough buss that occupied them for some time.

"Did you have fun getting fitted?" Max inquired, as he moved to sit on the edge of the bed, watching her finish fixing her hair and makeup, more intrigued by the woman than the process.

Finley turned to look at him, contour brush in hand. "Yeah. Whitt's dress is simply stunning. She's going to make such a beautiful bride." She returned her attention to the mirror, giving her cheeks one last touch-up.

"So would you," Max mused, his eyes betraying the sadness behind the half smile his lips gave her. Finley glimpsed the contradiction in his reflection and put her makeup brush down as she approached him.

"I'm as married as I ever need to be." She stood in front of him, her hands stroking his face, her gaze locked onto his. His hands moved to her waist.

"Are you sure?" The intensity of his eyes melted her, and her breath seized in her chest. He reached beside him for his phone and turned it toward her so she could see the image on the screen. "Exquisite, isn't she?"

It took a minute for Finley to divert her attention from Max's face to the picture. The woman in the shot wore an elegantly sculpted boatneck sheath in bright white. Her long coffee curls had been pulled into a loose chignon that showed her graceful neck and jawline to their advantage.

Finley laughed softly. "Where'd you get that?"

"Whitt sent it to me."

"The little sneak! Why would she do that?" Finley shook her head. "I thought it was Mama. I'm going to get her for that!"

"Why? I'm glad she sent it." Max pulled her onto his lap. "In all my imaginings, I never realized how breathtakingly beautiful you would be as a bride. Now I get to see!"

"What imaginings are these?" Finley shook her head in confusion. She would never understand how this man's mind worked. *What is he thinking? Does he want to get married? Is he dreaming of weddings now? I swear he needs therapy. Or I do!*

"One day, I'm going to get brave enough to ask you to marry me. One day." Max murmured into her ear, as he pushed her gently to her feet. "But now, we'd better go down before the others start speculating about what we're doing up here."

Officers Cabot and Horton came early the next morning to take Whitt's official statement. Whitt was still at a loss as to why it took two officers to take a three-line statement. In any event, they were gone as soon as they came, having no new information to share from their side as to the man's identity or his reason for being in their house. Whitt's pacing, and her rhetorical questioning of both the case investigation and her mother's preparations, had David worried.

"Her mind is working overtime trying to be the perfect hostess for people coming to the wedding—as well as trying to identify the body we found in the house. She even has me on edge!" David had lamented to Finley over dinner the previous evening. By morning, Finley had thought of a diversion.

"Who's up for the beach?" Finley proposed to the group, as they were finishing the breakfast dishes. "The weather's nice, and Mama doesn't have anything planned for us between now and Tuesday night when David's parents get in. I say we take advantage of it and go chill at the beach."

The rest of the crew was game. Within an hour, they piled into three cars and were off to Kiawah, one of the widest and flattest sand beaches on the East Coast, as far as Finley was concerned. Daddy was a founding member of the golf club there, so entry to the private beach was guaranteed. Mama had told Finley and Whitt that when she was growing up, the beach access had been a struggle. She recounted stories of the seemingly endless car or bus rides up to Atlantic Beach, near Myrtle Beach, to find shoreline on the ocean. More often than not, she and her sisters would just settle for Remleys Point on the Cooper River.

"I don't think it gets much better than this!" Logan exclaimed, as he spread out the blanket for Hema on an empty stretch of sand near Finley and Max's towels.

"You say that every time you visit a new place on the map!" Hema challenged.

Logan and Hema had met in Jaipur the previous year when Logan, a very wealthy entrepreneur who was a client of Mooney and, at the time, very FOF— Fond of Finley—had visited the sisters in India. Having established that romance between Finley and himself was off the table, he and Finley had instead established a deep friendship that was difficult for Max to understand initially. Over time, Logan and Max had reached a détente. More recently, David and Logan had entered into a partnership, introducing ancient wines from Central Asia to the American market.

"Maybe. But it is no less true just because it's true of many places!" Logan quipped, planting a sweet kiss on Hema's cheek before taking his place on the blanket.

Hema continued standing after the others had lain out in the sun or headed off to the water. "I am going shell searching before I get too settled. See you in a bit!"

Logan leaned back, using his backpack as a pillow, and followed her figure with his eyes until it was almost out of sight on the shoreline.

"You coming in?" Max asked Finley after Hema left.

"In a while. I think I want to enjoy the sun first. I'm guessing that water is cold this early in the season!" Finley responded, before he headed for a swim. She watched Max's long legs eat up the shore between the blanket and the water's edge. Within seconds, he waded in and submerged himself, coming up some distance from the beach.

"You two seem happy. Are you?" Logan shifted his gaze from the retreating dot that was Hema to that of Max in the surf. He then directed his eye to Finley.

"Very!" Finley beamed. She couldn't explain her sudden effusiveness, but she was truly, deeply satisfied with her life. She was looking forward to her sister's wedding, her life in London with Max, as well as the next assignment, wherever that was. "I'm really happy. And you? Are you and Hema the next ones down the aisle?"

"I would have thought it would be you and Max, but I see from the rings on both your finger and Max's that may have already happened!" Logan glanced at the wide, gold band on her ring finger. Shortly after he had placed the band on Finley's finger, Max had taken to wearing a simple platinum wedding band. He'd said nothing; he'd simply slipped it on and then never taken it off.

"Max has a thing about weddings, so we committed to each other instead. Almost a year ago." Finley thought back to that day and the feeling she'd had when he had promised to be hers forever. *It felt like home. It still does. No place in the world is safer than in his arms, his heart.*

"Congratulations! I'm so pleased for you. After seeing you two together in India, even when he was in a mood, I knew it was meant to be." Logan snickered at his recollection of Max in Jaipur in full jealous mode. "He would have fought me for you, you know! I was sure to lose."

"He was just having a rough time of it. He thought I was in love with every man but him, when that couldn't have been further from the truth!" Finley chuckled. "Even he laughs about it now!"

She looked at Logan. "But you still haven't answered my question about you and Hema."

"I think she and her family are wondering the same thing. We've been together almost a year. She has broken every rule about what a good Indian girl is supposed to do—traipsing around the world with me. With no chaperone—and no ring."

"Well?" Finley continued. "If you don't love her, Logan, you need to let her go."

"Don't love her? Good God! I adore her." Logan quickly pushed himself up on his elbow and turned to face Finley. His face softened, and an admiring smile inched up his lips. "I don't know that it's possible to love someone more!"

"Then what is it? Why haven't you asked her?"

"Actually, I was thinking of asking her this trip. After Whitt's wedding, of course. Wouldn't think of stealing your sister's thunder. Your mother would have me drawn and quartered if she even thought I might upstage her daughter."

"You got that right! Do have the ring picked out?"

Logan nodded sheepishly. "Yeah, I've collected the stones when we've traveled, based on what I see her looking at. I took a picture of an antique ring that she fell in love with at an auction in Rome and had it made in New York with a slightly larger stone. I think you'd like it—a European-cut center stone in a raised, filigree setting. Edwardian, as I recall."

"What's important is that she likes it, and I'm sure she will. I'm overjoyed for the two of you! She's a lucky girl!"

"No, dearest, I'm the lucky one!"

"That you are." Finley stood and stripped off her cover up. "I think I'm going to brave the frigid waters. I may be back sooner than I think."

"Max will keep you warm!" Logan joked and watched as she jogged into the water, giggling as the surf splashed up around her.

Finley swam out to where Max hovered, treading water. "So, you finally came in to do your polar bear plunge," he said, pulling her shivering body closer to him. "It warms up after a few minutes."

"I know, but those intervening minutes are torture."

"I'll warm you!"

Finley leaned in and kissed Max's cheek. "Logan said you would!"

"Did he now?" Max gave a crooked smile and wrapped an arm around her as they both flutter kicked to keep their heads above water. "What were you two talking about so intently?"

"You were watching us?"

"I always have an eye on you. Not to spy, but to keep you close," Max explained. "You have no idea how precious you are to me."

Finley leaned back to take in his face, his expression. So honest, so open. So vulnerable. Max rarely allowed himself to be so transparent. It was times like this when he did that she treasured above all others. She brushed her lips gently against his before coming back for a longer more thorough kiss.

"You're trying to drown us both!" Max teased when they pulled apart.

"I kissed you for less than a minute. You can hold your breath longer than that, can't you?"

"I don't know. Let's see." He pulled her in for another kiss. When they came up for air this time, they had been submerged for several seconds and had to push their way to the surface. They swam closer to the shore, stopping on a shelf in the ocean floor, where they could touch the bottom but still have some privacy.

"Where were we? Now, I can hold you properly." Max enveloped her in both of his arms and kissed her again fully. "Have I told you today how much I love you?"

"You may have, but I think I forgot. Can you remind me again, please?" Finley realized how much she enjoyed the casual, joking rapport she'd developed with Max over the past several months. The tension that had invaded their relationship at several junctures before their commitment was gone.

The day at the beach seemed to calm Whitt's nerves. She and the others walked back into Aunt Cora and Uncle John's house to find that the refrigerator had been restocked yet again—this time with pulled pork, barbequed chicken, coleslaw, and cornbread. A trifle and a sizable bowl of banana pudding had been put in the refrigerator as well.

In addition, there was a lemon buttermilk pound cake on the counter with a note from Aunt Cora that read, *I know your mama is going to overfeed you, but Mrs. Calhoun, who has known your mama and me since we were little girls, heard you girls were staying with me and had to send something over. You will be glad she did. Her cakes are divine! Enjoy, sweethearts!*

"If we keep eating like this, we won't be able to fit into our dresses!" Charlie commented, as she sliced a piece of the pound cake.

"Speak for yourself!" Kirsten joked. "Maternity clothes—especially those big enough to accommodate twins—are tents anyway! A little extra cake or banana pudding here and there won't alter the silhouette much. Just that of a bigger beached whale!"

"You don't look like a beached whale, baby," Reid offered. "At least, not yet!"

Kirsten playfully punched him before accepting his conciliatory peck on the lips. While the play fighting was going on, Whitt and David opened the Tupperware with the pulled pork, toasted a hamburger bun, and made themselves a plate of barbeque and slaw. David was licking sauce off his fingers when Finley left to pick up Daisy at Mama and Daddy's for a walk around the neighborhood. Max decided to tag along.

"I'll bet that poor puppy hasn't had a decent walk since we took her to the beach. Daddy is just too busy running around for Mama," Finley opined when she and Max walked into the backyard.

She threw up her hand in greeting at the clusters of family and neighbors that occupied the lawn chairs strewn around the pool and deck area. Why Mama had invited so many people for an open house so far in advance of the wedding was beyond Finley. Mama had remarked, through pursed lips, that it was necessary because of Whitt's insistence on such a small invitation list for the actual wedding.

"So many people want to help since they can't attend. You should be happy that they want to be involved in your special day!" Mama had declared.

Free food and drink for a week in exchange for stuffing bibelots into gift bags is more like it, Finley had thought. Whitt had wisely held her tongue.

With all the people running in and out of the gate, Daddy had attached Daisy's run line to the clothesline at the far side of the house. Away from most of the hubbub and traffic, the puppy had room to run without the risk of getting out of the gate and into the street. She darted toward Max and Finley when she caught sight of them, only to have the leash pull her up short when she got to the end of the clothesline.

"We'll spring you from this prison, baby girl," Finley cooed into Daisy's ear. "Let's go for a walk, sweetheart!"

At the word *walk*, Daisy dropped to a sit and waited until her walking harness had been attached. "She understands the word *walk*?" Max stared at the dog like she had spoken in tongues.

"Yes. She understands a lot of words. Once this wedding is over, I'll have Daddy show you just how well trained she is. She's young yet, but she's a smart girl. Aren't you?" Finley signaled a release and Daisy returned to puppy mode. Finley passed the leash to Max and let him walk her around the yard a few times to work off some energy. "Now you're ready to listen, eh, pretty girl!"

Finley took the leash and positioned Daisy on her left side. Immediately, Daisy picked up the cue and matched her stride to Finley's at the heel. When they went through the crush of visitors, Finley could sense Daisy's excitement, but the puppy maintained her control and stayed right by Finley's side. They were almost to the gate when Lael opened the side door of the house and stepped into the yard. Daisy stopped and inched her body closer to Finley. A barely audible, guttural growl started in Daisy's chest and settled in her throat. The hair on her spine prickled up, and her ears flattened.

"Hey, coz. Taking puppy for a walk?" Lael called out above the music that was playing in the background. "Good idea. Get her away from all this noise and madness. Enjoy your walk!"

Once on the sidewalk in front of the house, Finley relaxed the leash to let Daisy walk in front of her. Max moved beside Finley and took her hand as they followed behind the sniffing puppy.

"I don't think your dog likes your cousin much," he observed, after they were away from the house.

"You noticed that, too? Well, Daisy is in good company, because Whitt and I aren't too fond of her either!"

"So you said." Max chuckled. "I guess Daisy deserves a treat after her walk!"

They had barely gone two blocks before they saw a police car approaching. When the car stopped, Officer Cabot got out of the driver's seat. Officer Horton finished a call before joining her partner on the pavement.

"I'm glad we caught you away from the house. I get the impression your mama would prefer not to have cop cars in front of her house," Cabot stated. "We just wanted to let you know that you can move back into the Rutledge place now. We've completed our search of the house and have taken all the forensics. The owner okayed you guys heading back over. They'll send you a confirmation text. Enjoy the rest of your holiday and tell your sister congratulations."

It should be best wishes, Finley thought, but she wasn't going to argue. Whitt could start her wedding week in earnest now.

8

INLEY AND MAX SPENT THE last evening at Sullivan's watching the sunset over the marshes. After their conversation with Cabot and Horton, they'd sent one of the younger cousins over to the pool house at the Davises' with a note for Aunt Cora letting her know that they could move back into the house in Charleston and would be leaving in the morning. Finley also called the florist her mama always used and ordered a thank-you bouquet to be delivered to the Davises when they left. She then sent a text to her sister and asked her to inform the others. She could well imagine Whitt jumping for joy at the prospect of returning to her original wedding plans.

For her part, Finley wanted some alone time with Max. She loved the excitement and energy that being part of the wedding party brought, but she also missed her routine, especially the quiet time with Max, when they sat snuggled up, reading or watching TV together. After she'd fastened Daisy around back and given her some water and a treat, Finley took Max by the hand and led him into the house and up the stairs. She said nothing and simply smiled at the confusion on his face. His bafflement grew as she passed the second floor and headed to the third.

"Where are we going?" Max whispered, even though there was no one but Finley to hear.

"You'll see! Just wait," she replied.

On the third floor, Finley walked to a corner closet and retrieved a long-necked hook. With it, she snagged the O-ring that hung from a panel in the ceiling and pulled gently. A set of unrailed wooden stairs descended and rested on the hall floor.

"Are you going to take me to the attic and seduce me?" Max gave her a lopsided grin. "I won't say no."

Finley returned his smile but remained silent as she started her way up the stairs. She remembered when her Daddy had put these stairs in. It was the summer after the prank that had left the sisters locked out. Daddy hadn't made a fuss, hadn't demanded that Lael and Tommy apologize or promise never to do it again. He just made it so that they never could.

When she reached the top of the stairs, she paused. She could feel Max's presence behind her, but the view deserved its moment. After a minute, she stepped aside and drew Max onto the widow's walk. One side of the house threw its arms open wide to the great expanse of ocean that could be seen over the trees—shades of aqua and sea glass mixed with spots of cyan before melding into the horizon in a line of cerulean. On the other side, the marshes dominated, with the vibrant greens of the reeds and the derby browns of the cattails crowding either side of the silvery pathways of water that reflected an almost cloudless sky.

"It's going to be a really pretty sunset tonight. Clear skies," Finley murmured. "Thought you might like to see it."

Max simply nodded and pulled her onto the low bench that ran along the interior ledge of the platform. The sun had just started its descent into the horizon, painting the sky with splotches of tangerine and persimmon. The few clouds that hugged the skyline were blushed pink and capped in billowy white. The vista looked more like a painting than reality.

"Spectacular!" Max sighed when the sun had finally nestled itself under the covers of the horizon. The hush of twilight surrounded them. He'd wrapped his arms around Finley as they sat entranced by nature's nightly slow dance. As they waited and watched, she told him what her cousins had done on this widow's walk many years ago. He drew her close to protect her, savoring the warmth of her head on his chest, the quiet rhythm of her breathing, the comfort of her in his arms.

Finley raised her head and gently followed the curve of his upper lip with her fingertip. "We'd better go back down before Whitt has the National Guard looking for us."

Max leaned in and rested his lips on hers before getting to his feet, pulling her with him. They descended the stairs in raptured silence. When Finley had closed the stairs and returned the hook to its resting place, Max pulled her close and kissed her again. "Thank you for sharing this place, this time, with me. I don't know how it's possible, but I keep falling more in love with you every day."

Finley gave him a peck on the lips before leading him downstairs. "Good. Then maybe one day you will love me half as much as I love you!"

Finley didn't even bother telling Mama when they headed over to the Rutledge house the next morning. She had let both Mama and Daddy know when she sent the note over to Aunt Cora, so she saw little need for making a stop to say bye before they started the caravan over the bridge. Besides, it was Sunday. Mama and Daddy deserved to sleep in.

The Rutledge house bore no indication that anything untoward had ever occurred within its walls. The curtains had been thrown open to let in the morning light. Whitt and Finley unfastened the French doors that led to the sunroom and let the air flow freely around the downstairs of the house. Whitt started for the stairs and then stopped abruptly.

"You go first." Whitt pointed to the top of the stairs. "Make sure it's gone."

"Why me? I don't like bodies any more than you do," Finley retorted.

"Well, the guys are bringing in the bags. Kirsten can't. Charlie faints at the sight of blood—unless it's on an animal. And I am hardly going to ask Hema to do reconnaissance!" Whitt backed off the step to clear the way for Finley.

Finley cut her eyes at her sister as she mounted the stairs. "Which way, Miss Fraidy Cat?"

Finley could hear her sister's directions as she reached the top of the stairs and followed her instructions left and into the master bedroom. Finley had no idea what it had looked like when Whitt and David retreated to the safety of Sullivan's Island, but from what Finley could see, everything was in order. The room was tastefully decorated, just as the Airbnb photos had depicted. She slowly walked to the closet, standing before the closed doors an extra moment before quickly turning the latch and jumping back. When nothing fell out, she exhaled and turned to inspect the bathroom. She pulled back the shower curtain that surrounded the clawfoot tub, wholly expecting another body to be waiting there for her. Again, nothing.

"All clear, Whitt!" Finley called out.

"I see." Her sister's voice was close behind her. "Thanks for checking, just in case."

"Sure. I'm going upstairs to check out my room. I'll do a quick look in the other rooms to be sure. Hate for our guests to be traumatized!" Finley snickered. "A corpse under the covers might be enough to rupture a perfectly good friendship!"

While Whitt went down to direct Kirsten and Reid to their room, the only one on the ground floor, and tell David where upstairs to put Charlie's bag, Finley climbed the stairs to the next level. She opened the door to check Mooney and Ian's room before heading down the hall to hers and Max's. Upon entering, she paused. If she were an artist, this would be the perfect studio space. Broad shafts of sunlight poured in through the wide palladium window and pooled in the large sitting area at one end of the spacious loft. A love seat, an overstuffed reading chair, and a rectangular wood and metal coffee table populated that portion of the garret.

At the other end of the room, a mahogany sleigh bed snuggled under a featherweight linen canopy. The nonchalant melding of traditional features with modern accents made the space feel like one that Finley had lived in for years and was just returning to after a brief sojourn.

"Where do you want me to put these?" Max entered the room with two of their suitcases. "This is quite the place! You chose well, sweetheart."

Finley pointed Max and the bags to a small alcove off the dressing room that connected the bedroom to a lavish bathroom with marble counters and another clawfoot tub. "Thanks. I'm glad the reality matches with the pictures. You never know what you're going to get."

"You can say that again. I hope we don't have to pay extra for the 'additional' person that Whitt and David found bunking in their room!" Max sidestepped Finley to avoid her lighthearted jab.

"So, what are the others thinking of doing the rest of the day?" Finley asked, as she began to unzip the largest of her suitcases.

"Can't say for sure. I think Logan and Hema are heading to Callie's for more biscuits, and Kirsten and Reid are resting. I don't know about the others." Max started for the door. "I, for one, am going to take advantage of this great weather and the pool—after I grab the rest of the bags, of course."

"I'll likely join you and take advantage of the lull before Mama goes into full panic mode with David's parents and most of the other guests coming in. That isn't for another couple of days, but then the two of us are going to be on full Mama alert," Finley declared, as she hung her clothes in the spacious closet—no bodies in sight. "We need to keep Mama away from Whitt at all costs if we don't want her taking the next flight to Vegas! She's enough on the edge as it is!"

"Maybe we did do it the right way!" Max said, as he snuck a quick kiss before taking another look at the room. "I think I'm going to like our little love nest! Away from all the rest of the crew and any drama."

"Oh, I assure you, drama will find us if we don't manage Whitt!" Finley joked. "Let's just keep her busy. We'll leave David to do that today, while we rest up for the challenges of the rest of the week. Just pray there are no more dead bodies."

By the time Max and Finley had unpacked, the rest of the crew was downstairs in the den trying to come to some decision about lunch. Hema and Logan had struck out earlier on a self-guided tour of the city; Kirsten and Reid were still resting. That left David— who was hungry again—Whitt, and Charlie debating between eating in and going out. In the end, Whitt decided Charlie needed to experience more of the culinary charm of Charleston.

"Are you two coming with us?" Whitt asked. "We'll probably go to Poogan's."

Finley shook her head. "Nope. We'll nosh on whatever we brought over from Aunt Cora's. Max and I will probably just lie out by the pool. Have fun!"

"By the way, Cabot was here while you were upstairs unpacking. Came from church, all suited up with his family in tow. Cute little girl. Who'd have thought?" Whitt relayed. "He said they found the guy's car. His wallet was under the seat, so they were able to make an ID."

Whitt watched as David spooned trifle into a bowl. She got ready to remind him of the fact that they were on their way to lunch but stopped herself. He would still be looking for food by the time they got to the restaurant. She needn't worry.

"He said he stopped by Mama and Daddy's before he remembered we were likely over here. Luckily, he caught Daddy in the yard before he bothered Mama." Whitt chuckled at the earful Cabot would have gotten had he bothered Mama at the house, on a Sunday, no less.

David licked the last bit of cream from his spoon before rinsing it and putting it in the dishwasher. "He gave Whitt some serious grief for not recognizing her own cousin as the dead man."

"What? Who was it?" Finley approached Whitt, her brows knitted.

"Tommy!" Whitt replied.

"Tommy?" Finley echoed. "You didn't recognize Tommy?"

"Not you, too! Come on. Tell me you could recognize someone after ten years or more, especially half-jetlagged!" Whitt whined. "I haven't seen him since I was in high school. And back then he had hair and no beard!"

"I guess. Tommy…" Finley mused. "I never liked the guy, but I didn't wish him dead! Do they have any suspects?"

"No. Not that Cabot was sharing," Whitt concluded. "He said they would let us know as they got more information. So, I guess we're back to wedding mode."

Finley leaned over and planted a kiss on her sister's cheek. "Yes, baby sis. You can go full wedding prep crazy now, within reason though. No bridezilla stuff. But I suspect if you don't feed this boy soon, he's the one who'll be going crazy on you!"

Charlie and Whitt laughed at David, who had now cut a slice of cake. He looked up sheepishly. "Just to hold me over! You ladies kept talking, and I didn't want to interrupt and tell you to get going."

"Let's go!" Whitt giggled and grabbed her satchel and the car keys. "See you in a while!"

"No rush! We'll be here. Probably out back." Finley waved as she headed to the refrigerator to investigate the lunch options. "Enjoy!"

Shortly after Whitt, David, and Charlie left for lunch, Finley and Max changed into their swimsuits and headed to the pool, which took up much of the backyard. Unlike the massive infinity pool at the Sullivan's Island house, this was a dunk pool, long and relatively shallow, running down the middle of the narrow yard. The old trees that had been left guarding the two extreme corners of the space provided a leafy umbrella, filtering the midday sun that was inching the thermometer up.

Max poured each of them a glass of a salmon-colored rosé from Provence while Finley pulled together a plate of assorted snacks—slices of ham, wedges of cheese, gherkins, a small pot of pimento cheese, crackers, and cheese straws.

"There's still some banana pudding in there. I may not be able to resist," Finley commented. "I'm surprised that Whitt didn't recognize Tommy when she saw him at the airport. But then again, it has been years—no, decades—since we saw each other. And a beard and bald head will change your appearance!"

"Well, you sisters have one of the widow's walk culprits out of the way. Now to deal with Lael!" Max said conspiratorially.

"You're horrible!" Finley exclaimed. "We just wanted them out of our lives, not out of this earthly realm!"

Max and Finley spent the rest of the afternoon sprawled out, reading on the patio lounge chairs. In time, Kirsten and Reid came to join them. Kirsten had slipped on a floral one-piece bathing suit with a flouncy little peplum that accommodated her belly and still afforded her some signature sass.

"You have a nice rest?" Finley inquired. "There's some iced tea in there. And still gobs of food—both sweet and savory, depending on what you're craving. Are you having cravings?"

"Thanks. We'll get something in a minute. No real cravings that weren't there before I got pregnant. I can put a hurtin' on a tub of mocha almond fudge ice cream. Always could," Kirsten shared. "But now, the only thing I miss is alcohol. I must have alcoholic tendencies. I'll crave a real drink and then sit and sniff Reid's hoping to get a contact high!" Finley got a visual of poor Reid mixing up martinis and watching his wife inhaling the vapors in a euphoric trance.

The whole crew was around the pool when Lael stopped by later. Hema and Logan had returned from their touring and lunch with several shopping bags. They had dropped their purchases in their room before grabbing glasses of a crisp Virginia Viognier Whitt had gotten a couple of days earlier at a local wine store on East Bay. By the time the wine had been poured, the wine purveyor herself, with husband-to-be and best friend in tow, rolled in. Whitt, too, had shopping bags, which David carried up the stairs to their room.

"Did you guys have a good time?" Finley asked, as the crew settled in to wine and cheese. They were in the midst of sharing tales of their afternoon exploits when Lael came through the back gate.

"Hey, y'all! I rang the buzzer, but no one answered, and then I heard the buzz back here." She sashayed in, wearing a white A-line sundress with powder-blue flowered wedges. Her long, fawn-colored locks were perfectly blown out, even this late on a Sunday afternoon, and her makeup was skillfully applied to emphasize her amber eyes. *She looks like a Barbie doll—almost as waxen!* Finley thought before reprimanding herself for her cattiness. She stole a glance at her sister, whose mouth was puckered like she had eaten Sour Patch candies.

Finley stood to greet her cousin, the only polite response. "Come on in! We're just enjoying a lazy Sunday afternoon. Can we get you something to drink?" Finley asked, ushering Lael in. "I think you've met everyone."

"Yes," Lael drawled, elongating the one syllable response to two. "So nice to have you come into town. I just stopped by to be sure you were all okay and settling in. So sorry about the unfortunate circumstances that greeted you, Whitt! But it looks like it's all been taken care of." She turned to look toward the interior of the house.

Whitt and David both nodded. Whitt sat, eying her cousin the way you would a rattler that was coiled but not striking—wary and ready to run. David didn't know this woman, but something about her didn't sit right with him. He moved to stand behind Whitt.

Lael continued in an animated voice. "And your mama told me it was poor Tommy who was in that bag! I went over to the house with my mama this morning and heard. That is a crying shame! I didn't know him well, at least not lately, but well . . . we were cousins."

What in God's name were you and your mama doing back over at the house? Finley wondered, but she put the thought out of her mind and plastered on a concerned look that she hoped wasn't as artificial as it felt. "Yes, it is a shame. I wonder what he was doing in the house in the first place. I guess we'll never know!"

"Truly," Lael uttered in response, before picking up a large, floral-patterned tote that she had rested on the table as she conversed. "Well, I had better get out of here. Sundays are a realtor's best day, you know. And I have an open house that starts in another hour."

Finley stood again to escort her to the gate. "So glad that you stopped by. Sorry you couldn't stay longer," Finley intoned. "And I love that bag! It looks great with your outfit!"

"This old thing? I pulled it out to wear with a dress I had on earlier in the week and just forgot to change bags. It had a couple of smaller pouches that went with it, but goodness knows where those went. You know how these things are. I'll find it one day where I least expect it!"

Lael leaned in and gave Finley a quick kiss on the cheek before throwing up her hand at the rest of the group. "Enjoy your day!"

Finley waited at the gate until Lael had driven off. *I really don't like that woman. Here she was trying to be polite and hospitable, and I'm scoffing at her every word. And Whitt's no better. We should be ashamed!*

Finley had just picked up her wine glass when her phone rang. Officer Horton's voice was on the other end. "This is Officer Horton. Sorry to bother you and your family again on a Sunday, but we are perplexed by something and are hoping you might be able to help."

Finley listened in silence to the officer's request before indicating her agreement and ringing off.

"What was that about?" Whitt queried her sister.

"Horton was asking if we could look around again for a set of keys. Seems they found Tommy's wallet in his car, but they can't locate his keys for the car or house anywhere. They're puzzled at how his car got to where it was found, on some back road a few miles out of town, without the keys."

"He might've run out of gas or had car problems and hitched back into town with the keys. And just forgot to get his wallet from under the seat," Whitt conjectured.

"Yeah. But then it seems the keys would have been on his person when he was found, and they weren't," Finley countered. "And the police have been all over this house. They are asking that we look for anyplace they might be dropped or hidden as we wander the grounds. I said we would keep an eye out."

"Not a very promising investigation," Max concluded. "You ladies are back sleuthing again!"

9

MAMA HAD EVERYONE WHO WAS going to Beaufort up and out at the crack of dawn. As much as Whitt wanted to take a pass on the trip, Mama insisted that both Whitt and Finley go, which meant David and Max felt compelled to accompany them or be labeled as lackadaisical young men. Daddy was taking the Rover so it could fit the six of them; anyone else who wanted to go would have to trail behind. As it turned out, the others treasured their sleep and opted to find entertainment for the day on their own.

"I haven't been to the Beaufort house in years. Not since after Mom died." Mama's voice had softened to a whisper when she mentioned her mother. Mama was quite surprised when Mom left the little house in Beaufort to her. Each of the sisters had gotten property, but this house had been the first one that Mr. Harland had bought for Miss Charlotte—as most people called Finley and Whitt's grandmother—after they were married. While Grandaddy was from Greensboro, across the border in North Carolina, he knew better than to take his young bride away from her family and bought the house in Beaufort so she could be closer to kin.

Frequently overshadowed by its big sister Charleston, Beaufort was a picturesque port city in its own right, with stately mansions populating its palm-lined streets. The state's second-oldest city, located some seventy miles down the coast from Charleston, was named for the second Duke of Beaufort. It had flourished during the antebellum era, when it became a summer retreat for wealthy rice planters.

"Mama said you started repairs on the place, Daddy." Whitt sat on the bench seat behind Daddy, her arm wrapped through David's. He played with the fingers of her hand, which he held in his. "What are you having done?" she asked.

Daddy glanced in the rearview mirror. "Right now, just the roof, which we knew was falling in. That's partly why your mama wants to go out now. To figure out what else needs to be done so we can take care of it while we're down home this time."

Finley smiled. She suspected Daddy was as confused about where "home" was as she was. At least he was only plagued by two choices—the house in Chevy Chase or the place on Sullivan's. Finley doubted that either Mama or Daddy considered the house in Beaufort home. When Mama's mother died and Mama took over the house, she and Daddy came down and cleaned it up, getting it ready for rent. They initially rented it to a couple, but soon it was only the man living there. And now the man had stopped paying his rent, despite many calls, first from Daddy and then from Daddy's lawyer.

Daddy pulled up to the house. It had an appealing aura to it, like something out of a storybook. It was a compact bungalow with twin dormers and a covered entry. The shingles were painted white, with dark-blue shutters for accents. The little porch had a proper haint-blue ceiling and a white rollback bench swing on one side. The stone pavers that led to the front door had some stones missing, making the house look a little worn and snaggletoothed. The white picket fence that outlined the property was in good enough shape to keep the place just on this side of lived-in instead of inching toward dilapidated.

"Good gracious. This place looks like it's seen better days." Mama had gotten out of the car and stood on the sidewalk in front of the house, staring at it, hands on hips, while she assessed just how bad the situation was. She was glad that the guys working on the roof had taken special care not to damage the azaleas and camelias that encircled the house as foundation plantings. Her visage grew sterner as her assessment of the house progressed.

Finley remembered being on the receiving end of that look more times than she could count. It was the one Mama gave you when you came down for dinner out wearing something that she had hoped you wouldn't put on. Rather than just ask you to change, Mama would stand there, scrutinizing the outfit, head tilted slightly to the side, mouth twisted, eyes examining every detail of the dress or pants or jacket. After a few excruciating minutes of inspection, Finley would give in and ask Mama what she'd prefer she wore.

"What are you thinking, Kat?" Daddy now stood beside Mama, joining in giving the sweet little house the once-over. "Before we go in and see what needs doing inside, what do you want to do to increase the curb appeal? We might as well bite the bullet now, if you want to renovate, since nobody's in it."

"I understand, dear. But I also don't want this to be a money pit." Mama leaned over and gave Daddy a peck on the cheek. "I know you want to do right by Mom and Dad's house, but let's not go overboard. I think repainting, fixing the pavers, and some land-scaping will suffice for the outside."

Daddy put his arm around her shoulders. "If you're sure, then let's head on in."

The house had been closed up for several months, Mama said. Neither she nor Daddy knew how long Mr. Elijah Hale had lived in the place after he ceased paying rent, but they were expecting layers of dust and dirt. Instead, they found the living and dining area not much different than if the tenant had simply been away on a two-week vacation. The plants on the windowsill had withered, and there was some mail on the entry hall floor, having been pushed through the slot by the mail carrier before Daddy asked that the tenant's mail be held at the post office. Aside from that, the place was pristine.

"Mr. Hale appears to have been a tidy man," Mama commented. "Thank heavens for that. It looks like the interior has been very well maintained."

She and Daddy wandered into the kitchen. The counters were free of clutter, all the dishes in their place. Even the dishwasher had been emptied and a small container of coffee grounds placed on the floor of the machine. The place had been rented fully furnished with everything, including dishes and linens. Mama knew for sure that the sheets and towels would need to be replaced even if the dishes and glasses were still usable.

While Daddy and Mama inspected the three bedrooms, the Four Musketeers, as Finley, Whitt, Max, and David called themselves, opened the door that led to the backyard. They had to push through the tarps that shrouded the rear roofline and part of the house. Even though the roof repairs were still in progress—only just beginning, from the looks of things, in fact—Finley could envision what the house would look like when it was all repaired and cleaned up.

The backyard landscaping had survived neglect better than the front yard had. In fact, it looked like it had thrived with a bit less pruning and clipping. The summer climbing roses had twisted themselves around the lattice and had used some errant morning glories as a trellis to reach the clothesline. There, the morning glory vines and the fragrant roses had intertwined and were creating an improvised arch across the edge of the garden.

"It reminds me of the book *The Secret Garden*!" Whitt remarked. "These roses are absolutely gorgeous. If I tried in a million years, I couldn't get them to grow this lushly."

"It is a peaceful little space. Like a quaint, English cottage garden," Max added, taking a whiff of a nearby rose. "Who lives here?"

"Lived, as in past tense. I really don't know. I know there were renters for a while and when they stopped paying, Daddy had to go after them. Besides that, I'm clueless," Whitt responded.

"This would be a cute place for us to live, if we were based in the States," David considered. "Just the right size. What's the town like?"

Whitt stared at David, pausing for a moment or two before answering. "Beaufort is a pretty little town with a lot of history, but it's small. Really small, especially compared to Charleston, and Charleston isn't really that big. Why?"

"Just wondering." David walked a few paces to the far end of the yard and looked back at the house. "With a little work, it really could be a nice house!"

"You could live here?" Whitt was bewildered by the conversation. She knew David knew that a condition of her getting married was that they would continue to live the expat life. Coming back to the US wasn't in the cards for a long time out—and coming to live in a small town wasn't in the cards at all.

As she stood trying to process a reaction to a possible life in small-town USA, David reached over and took her hand. "I know you've got a bad case of wanderlust. And frankly, so do I. But there may come a time when a slower, more settled pace suits us. And a little country cottage like this might be fun!" He drew her close and gave her a reassuring kiss. "No time soon, though. No time soon."

Finley and Max watched the exchange from the shade of the improvised rose arbor. They had never really discussed where they would live. Projects had dictated where they landed. Most recently, it had been India, and Morocco before that. London was where Max's things were, where he had planted himself as a permanent expat. But only until the next project came along, and then that would be where they lived. Finley had made Manhattan home when she'd been with the consulting firm, but when she left on assignment, New York was just a place she stored most of her clothes. Even so, she and Max never really discussed it, except to decide when to leave and how long they would be staying in the next place.

"Could you live here?" Max must have read her mind. That was the question she was getting ready to ask him.

"You beat me to it. So, I'll answer, and then you have to respond to the same question." Finley pondered. "I think so, but I'm not sure. If you asked me that when we were standing in an English country garden or a French village, I would have said yes in a heartbeat. But I'm less certain about this house and this town. Give me St. Michaels or Watch Hill, if it's in the US. Down here, I think I'd need a bigger town."

"Interesting. You always surprise me!" Max smiled.

"How? What did I say that surprised you?"

"That you could live in a small town. I would've had you as a city girl. I'd have thought that Charleston would be as small as you could get."

"You're right, for the most part, but I like walks in the country. I could live on a small farm or in a cottage with a garden. I like dirt, and sometimes a flower box doesn't do it for me."

"I will keep that in mind." Max kissed the inside of her wrist. "Whatever makes you happy!"

"I'm so glad my happiness is your quest, kind sir. Now, your turn. Could you live in a small town? Either here or elsewhere in the world?"

"Yes. I'd love a cottage in the Cotswolds, with climbing roses and cutting flowers and a babbling brook nearby."

"And sheep and horses in the meadow?"

Max nodded. "Are you in my country reverie, too? It needs a fair maiden."

"I told you, wherever you are, I am." Finley kissed him lightly before circling back for a second round. When she opened her eyes, her daddy was standing in the doorway, shaking his head with a grin.

"Can't leave you young'uns alone for a minute without you getting into a mess. Kissing and snuggling in public! What's the world coming to?" he joked, as he stepped back inside. "Your mama wants you."

When they walked back into the house, Mama was at the dining room table, mapping out the repairs and renovations that needed to be done. "I'm thinking that the whole house, inside and out, is ready for a lick of paint. Keep with the white outside, and maybe a pale gray in the inside common areas."

She looked up to check the expressions on the faces of the gathered group. Seeing no violent objections, she continued. "For the kitchen, I think the same gray walls with stark white cabinets and a new backsplash." Mama paused for a minute and went back over her notes. "I was thinking a blue-gray in the bedrooms, but now I think it's best to just carry the gray throughout. What do you think?"

Daddy, despite being an architect and designer, just shrugged. David and Max smiled, more in acknowledgement than agreement. Finley simply nodded. Whitt was the only one that spoke up.

"Mama, you sure you don't want to go with a pale yellow on the outside, instead of the white? All the other houses on the block are white. This one needs to stand out. And I like the gray throughout to tie the rooms together since it's a small house, but you might want to play with the shades of gray you use. Like maybe a darker gray in the common areas and a lighter one in the bedrooms," Whitt offered.

Mama turned in her chair to face her younger daughter. "I like the gradients of gray in the inside, and I love the yellow!" Her face broke into a wide grin. She stacked her notes and drawings and stuck them into her pocketbook. "The only thing we will need to check is what color the azaleas in the front are. We wouldn't want them to clash with the yellow paint color!"

Daddy, sensing that Mama was ready to take her leave, went to the back door and closed it firmly, turning and checking the lock. Mama had started for the door when the crew heard a slow screech that, within seconds, grew into to a yawning creak.

"What in goodness name is that?" Mama asked, turning back to look at her husband. "Is that the floors or the roof? We need to add 'check the foundation' to the list."

Mama was almost to the dining room when the creak began to crackle and debris started sprinkling down from the ceiling. Before anyone could react, the house groaned, and the ceiling split open and crashed to the living room floor in a mushroom cloud of dust. When the dust cleared, Finley, Whitt, and the rest stood staring at an oversized, green, Army-issue duffle bag. The side of the bag ripped—perhaps from the impact, perhaps from age—exposing its contents. A brittle partial skeleton.

1 0

DADDY GOT TO MAMA JUST in time to save her from hitting the floor. The crew gulped as they watched Mama's knees buckle and her head loll back. Daddy crossed the floor in two strides and gathered Mama in his arms. He carried her over to a dustcloth-draped sofa and sat down with her in his lap. Max went to the kitchen and returned with a glass of water.

"Finley, baby, go to the car and look in the hunter's bag in the back. There should be a flask and some supplies in there. Just bring the bag," Daddy directed.

Before Daddy could finish the request, Finley was out the door and down the walk. She came back in with a leather courier-looking bag in which she found a flask. She opened it, using the tail end of her tunic to wipe the lip of the flask. *Who knows whose lips have been on this thing. The people Daddy hunts with are not the most hygienic-looking creatures.*

Daddy smiled at the gesture, taking the vessel and raising it to Mama's lips. When she saw Mama's head recoil at the strong vapors of the bourbon, Finley knew Mama would come around. Finley's eye met her sister's, and they both moved closer to the body—or, more accurately, the bones.

They silently scanned the bag. Camouflage green. Seemingly Army issue or at least Army surplus. There was a faded name on the side that was now illegible. *Who did this belong to? How long has it been there? And how long has it been stuffed with a body? How long does it take for a body to revert to just bones? How long has this body been here? And, more importantly, who put it there—this last tenant or the one before? Was that whose name was on the bag?* Finley's mind was working. She could see her sister following the same train of thought. Finley nodded toward the front door, and the two slipped out.

"We need to call the police, and then we can talk," Finley stated.

"You call them this time! I've already done my civic duty with the call I made to them about the last body," Whitt argued.

Finley chuckled and dialed 911. After she reported the finding to the desk officer, she headed back into the house, leaving Whitt on the sidewalk to flag them down. She signaled David to join Whitt outside, then she moved to stand beside Max, who had resumed his guard position over the dusty duffle bag. Daddy was plying Mama with a few more sips from the flask and talking to her in a low, soothing voice. After another sip, Mama nodded and leaned her head on Daddy's shoulder.

"Your mother seems to be coming back to life. No pun intended," Max whispered. "Did you guys call the police?"

Finley's head dipped in acknowledgement even as her eyes went back to the debris that had fallen from the ceiling. Along with the duffle bag, a small suitcase, insulation, and several black garbage bags—the sort of things one might normally find in an attic—had fallen from the rafters. The only unusual items were the bones, which were sticking through black plastic. A few scraps of cloth were visible through the open seams. *Were those on the body or packed in the bag?* Finley was itching to open the bag and see what other clues might be hidden, but she knew better than to disturb a crime scene. Instead, she approached her mother.

"Mama, you feeling better?" Finley queried gently. "You had quite a scare!"

Mama slid off her husband's lap and onto the sofa. She touched the cover sheet tentatively and, finding no visible dust, relaxed her shoulders. Her eyes softened as she looked up at her daughter. "Yes, baby, I'm fine. Where's your sister?"

"Outside, waiting for the police."

"Oh dear, more police. This is not at all the morning I had planned for us! That poor child. Not the best wedding week!"

"It'll be fine, Mama. Once they take our statements, we can get back to the wedding prep. David's parents come in tonight, and Whitt will be distracted by that. Max and I will handle as much of the police inquiry as we can so that you and Whitt can focus on the wedding." As she was talking, Finley came to recognize the potential complexities of distracting both her mama and her sister in the midst of two murder investigations. *I think I need that flask!* Finley contemplated.

Whitt showed two police officers into the compact living room. Daddy had opened the back door so that the room didn't feel so tight and claustrophobic. One of the officers was a large refrigerator of a man with a blondish-red bowl haircut, and the other a man of average build who looked slight in the shadow of his partner. They introduced themselves before taking a look at the rubble on the floor. The larger officer reached into the metal suitcase he had brought in, pulled out a camera, and started snapping pictures.

Finley realized with a start that she had taken almost no pictures this trip. She hadn't had time. From the start of her stay in Charleston, she had been distracted by Tommy's murder, the craziness of the wedding, and the growing cadre of houseguests. Her typical refuge behind the camera had been put aside to deal with the chaos going on around her. Still, it felt unnatural. In the coming days, her camera would have to wait yet again while she managed Whitt and Mama as the wedding got closer.

Finley and Whitt flanked their mama on the sofa as Daddy took the police through the events of the previous hour. David and Max sat at the dining table and listened. Daddy recounted that the last tenant had stopped paying rent and that he and Mama had come down to Beaufort to check on the house after several years of renting it. He introduced his daughters and their partners before replaying the movements of the party since they'd arrived.

"Do any of you know who this might be?" the slighter officer asked, pointing to the bones and surveying the room as he carefully phrased the question. The assembled shook their heads.

"Well, we'll finish processing the scene and then let you lock up and go. Please do not leave the state. Let us know if you are going anywhere other than your respective places of current residence." He passed a card to Daddy and then to each of the others. "Please give us a call if you remember anything. Nothing is too small."

The group stayed in place while the officers finished taking pictures and then began to sort through the debris on the floor. In gloves and masks, the two policemen first unzipped the duffle and pulled out the black bag that the bones were wrapped in. Scraps of blue-and-white patterned material fluttered between the bone fragments as they were placed in evidence bags. After searching and bagging items from the duffle, the officers moved to the things on the floor, many of which were buried under mounds of insulation fibers. *Hope that's not asbestos. Those guys have on masks, but we don't!* Finley considered.

The larger officer pushed insulation off one of the several garbage bags that had fallen and grabbed it by the neck. As he lifted it, however, the bag burst open and several ziplocked bags spilled to the floor.

"Damn! One more thing we have to clean up," the officer blurted out before turning, shamefaced, to the women on the sofa. He lowered his eyes in Mama's direction. "Sorry, ma'am."

He began to gather the fifteen or so clear plastic bags in a mound. He opened one of the pint bags near the top, pushing back the wrapper to see the contents.

"Ned, you gotta see this," he gulped, still staring into the Ziploc. His partner leaned over and looked into the bag. He drew a breath and then raised his head slowly, leveling his gaze at Daddy. Before he could speak, the larger officer drew his attention again.

"There's more! A lot more!" he rasped.

The officer called Ned straightened up. "Do you want to tell us about this?"

Daddy stood and walked over to the officers. "About what? Wha—" Daddy stopped midsentence. "What the hell… where did this come from?"

"We were hoping you could tell us, General," Ned responded, his brow arched in question, a smirk dancing around his lips.

Daddy drew himself up to his full size, more than matching the height of the larger officer and dwarfing the officer who had addressed the comment to him. His voice echoed in the room even though he barely spoke above a whisper. His articulation of each word was as sharp as the crease in his trousers. "As I indicated before, neither my wife nor I have been to this house in over five years. My daughters and their partners have never been here before. I have no idea where that money came from. Given the volume, it appears to have been accumulating for some time. I think you have a puzzle to figure out, gentlemen. But you aren't going to solve it looking at us."

Ned and the other officer quickly got Daddy's message. The smirk now gone, Ned responded, "Yes, sir, we do have investigating to do. Tom, open the other bags and see if there's more. Then bag it up. Call over and see if we can't get another couple guys to help us, so we can search this place and get these folks out of here."

Finley got up so Daddy could sit beside Mama. She pulled out a dining chair near Max. He reached over and wordlessly took her hand. She cast him a glance and a shy smile, which was met with a squeeze of her hand followed by a light kiss on her fingers. Comforted, she turned her eyes back to the tallying of the money bags.

When the other garbage bags were opened, only one other contained money. Like the first, it held ziplocked bags of various sizes stuffed with bundles of money, bound together with rubber bands and wrapped in paper towels or black construction paper. The officers estimated about $15,000 in total.

"Good God!" Mama exclaimed when the estimate was thrown out. "Why ever wouldn't you put that much money in the bank?"

The two officers looked at each other before responding. "Ma'am, criminal elements prefer not to use banks. I suspect this was ill-found gain. We'll find out soon enough. We'll put an officer out here to see who comes back for it. They aren't likely to leave this much money behind."

"I guess that means the roof repairs—and everything else—are on hold!" Mama said, looking at Daddy. "Is nothing going to go as planned?"

Officer Ned looked contrite. "Sorry, ma'am, but we don't have a choice. We are treating this as a murder scene."

Daddy patted Mama's hand and looked past her to Whitt. This whole time, Whitt hadn't uttered a peep. Periodically, she had caught David's eye; he had offered an encouraging smile as the search of the house continued. Finley watched her sister's face. Whitt's eyes focused on the officers' every movement, her brow furrowed in concentration, her tongue distractedly tracing the contours of her upper lip. *She is trying to figure this out. She's probably wondering if there's a connection to the body she and David found. I'd hazard not. Different time frame and different place. But who knows?*

When the two additional officers arrived, they proceeded to the attic, where they found three more garbage bags, two of which held money. Besides that, the space was empty. Most everything else had fallen through the hole in the ceiling.

"Was there a robbery that these might be tied to?" One of the officers asked when the bags were brought down and placed with the others. "I mean, this could be an old lady's savings, but I don't think so."

After the bags were dusted for prints, the officers gathered the contents and placed them inside another garbage bag that was zip-tied and labeled. After what seemed like hours, the officers began to take the bags out to their vehicles.

"We're sorry to have kept you so long, but we wanted to be thorough. We'll take all of this down to the station. The house will be sealed off now, so we'll ask you to please proceed to your car. One of my officers will have to do one last check of your belongings, as a precaution. Apologies again."

As they filed out in pairs, one of the junior officers checked their handbags and satchels. When they got to the car, Daddy threw the hunter's bag back into the trunk and climbed into the driver's seat.

"I don't know about you, but I could use a drink." Daddy threw a glance over at his wife, who had rested her head on the back of the seat.

"And David is probably long overdue for some food," Whitt noted, kissing her fiancé's cheek.

David, wanting to be certain that he didn't make light of the situation they'd just witnessed, jumped in. "Look, I'm fine. Whatever Mrs. Blake is up for. It's been a tough day."

Mama pulled herself upright and touched Daddy's arm gently. "Let's go get you that drink and feed our groom back there. I could use a glass of wine now that you mention it. Whatever is this world coming to! Two murders in less than two weeks!"

When Daddy pulled the car into the graveled driveway of a boutique hotel, the sisters were surprised. Mama generally avoided hotel restaurants like the plague. *This one must have a Michelin star or a special bourbon that Daddy likes,* Finley figured. *Whatever. I think I'm going to join Daddy in that bourbon, and I'll bet Max goes with whiskey.*

Mama sashayed through the lobby, nodding greetings as she went. When she reached the dining room, which was only half full, she paused. The maître d' scurried over to greet her, planting kisses on both cheeks.

"Mrs. Blake. General. So glad to see you again. And with your family, I presume?" the man gushed, taking in the foursome with whom he was not acquainted. Mama politely went through introductions. The pleasantries addressed, the maître d', Claude, swiftly led them to a table on the wide balcony that extended the entire back of the building. "Does this suit you? I thought you might like a view of the water."

Mama gave a queenly nod as Claude pulled out her chair. Once everyone was seated, he gave an imperceptible sign, and the service began. Waitstaff came to arrange napkins, pour water, and bring menus and a wine list. Within seconds, they had come and gone, and the group was left to ponder the choices.

In the end, Finley, Whitt, and Mama split a bottle of champagne, a Roederer Cristal, while Daddy convinced Max to try his favorite aged bourbon, a sixteen-year-old Taylor sour mash, instead of Max's usual Macallan 18. Knowing David's preference for a good red, he recommended a classic cabernet sauvignon.

Daddy watched David's face light up with his first mouthful of the red. David exhaled and shook his head in awe when he reached the wine's finish. Daddy then turned to Max to see his reaction to the mellow whiskey he was sipping. Max had taken the bourbon into his mouth and was considering its warmth on his tongue. Finley knew the routine, having seen him experience his beloved single malts. She figured he would approach bourbon the same way. It appeared that he would. As the caramel liquid ran down his throat, a wry smile inched up his face.

"Nice," was his breathy response to Daddy's silent query. "Very nice!"

Finley reached over and took the glass from Max's hand, breathing in the rich vanilla fragrance before taking a sip. She sucked in a little air so that her mouth was full of the layered flavors emitted by the bourbon. She waited for the burn when she swallowed but felt none. *Smooth. Very smooth. Like drinking silk.* She liked this one. A lot. *And well you should. At this price point, you better love every little thing about it.*

"What'd you think, girl?" Daddy asked, eying her with a smile.

"Tastes like more."

"Well, I can get you one! You can let your mama and sister finish the champagne."

"Naw, that sip was enough. I'll go back to my Cristal," Finley replied.

She passed the glass to Max and stole a kiss in the process. "Thanks," she whispered.

"For what? The bourbon or the kiss?" Max murmured, aware they were being observed.

"Both," Finley mouthed, picking up her champagne flute and taking a sip. The bubbly stood up well to the whiskey taste that lingered on her lips.

"Glad you two like the Taylor. I considered getting the Van Winkle, but it was an older one, and I like the younger ones for flavor. This one has both—the smoothness and the taste."

Mama accepted Daddy's offer to top up her glass of champagne. "I, for one, am just glad that you children take it neat." She recalled Pappy Van Winkle saying it was better to add whiskey to water than the other way around. "That way you make a poor thing better rather than a fine thing worse."

Mama continued. "The woman that owned the house before John and Cora bought it—Dr. Edward's wife. You know the one. Sold the house to the Davises before her husband was even cold in the ground and moved back North. Anyway, she always took hers with water and ice." Mama rolled her eyes, giving the woman the "bless your heart" kiss of death. "And they wonder why the South continues fighting the War Between the States to this day. The North keeps watering down our bourbon. Pure sacrilege!"

Max was midswallow and almost spit his bourbon across the room upon hearing Mama's comment. Luckily, he caught himself, but he had to swallow hard to keep from choking. David paused as he lifted his glass to his lips and glanced over at Whitt to see if his future mother-in-law was serious or not. Understanding from Whitt's expression that she was indeed serious, he carefully placed his glass on the table and sat back in awe. This was going to be an interesting acculturation for him. It was easier being an expat overseas than it was being at sea in a subculture of a country that was supposed to be your home. Maybe he had been abroad too long.

"Before our food comes, can someone tell me what was going on at that house today?" Mama leaned forward, wide-eyed, speaking in a hushed voice so that the few other diners on the terrace couldn't hear. "Bodies falling from the ceiling. And then all that money! Do you think our tenant was running drugs or something?"

Finley cut a tickled glance at Whitt before she could catch herself. Her mama talking murder! At the table, no less! Now that was a new one! Mama was normally the one putting the Southern kibosh on talking, in polite company, about anything that smacked of death. Whitt caught the irony, too, and had to stifle a giggle.

"Could be, sweetheart. From what we saw, he should have had more than enough money to pay the rent," Daddy responded.

Whitt's demeanor changed quickly when she realized the implications of what Daddy said. "So does the fact that he didn't pay rent mean that he's dead?" she whispered, her eyes matching Mama's.

"But those aren't his bones, if he is dead, unless someone has been paying his rent for him for a while," Finley interjected. "It would likely take a year or more around here for bones to dry like those were, and he had been paying rent up until six months ago. So, I don't think that's him. It's someone else."

"So, we may have another body that has yet to be identified?" Max asked, his brows knitting together. "That is a lot of murder for such a small town. Does this happen often?"

Daddy laughed. "We don't have many murders around here. At least, I haven't heard of many. This is an aberration, for sure."

"What it also might suggest is that these murders are connected," Finley asserted, just as their meals were served. Despite her earlier curiosity, Mama's look put an end to any further murder conversation.

11

DADDY DROPPED THE MUSKETEERS OFF at the Rutledge house after lunch, leaving them all of the afternoon and much of the evening before David's parents arrived. The two sets of parents, especially the mothers, had spoken often since Whitt and David's engagement was formally announced.

While both families knew the wedding would happen in Charleston, it wasn't until the couple's trip to the Taj Mahal almost a year ago that David had made it official, and they had set the date. He'd asked Whitt for her hand in marriage several months before, but, in Whitt's inimitable way, it had become complicated by the conditions she'd imposed on the nature of their life together once married. David had readily agreed to all her conditions and had dropped to one knee in front of the Taj Mahal to seal the deal.

Whitt and Finley could sense Mama's excitement over meeting the Quinns, especially Ellie, David's mother. So much so that Daddy and Mama were heading to the airport to pick them up from their California flight.

"You really don't have to do that," David had protested. "Whitt and I can run out and get them."

Mama had stood firm. "It's not a problem. Besides, it may be our only chance to have a real conversation with them, given all the people running in and out of the house between now and the wedding. They're going to be staying over at Cora and John's. Less noise and distraction."

Whitt had signaled to David that the decision had been made and he was whistling into the wind if he thought he could change her mind. Whitt turned her attention to being sure that Mooney's room was ready for her. *Don't want the new beau thinking her friends, even if once removed, are flighty and can't keep house.* Whitt stopped herself midthought. *Good Lord, I sound like Mama. And it isn't even my house to keep.*

Mama summoned Finley over to the Sullivan house midafternoon for a food run. She and Max made the fifteen-minute ride over the bridge to load up the Rutledge house with provisions for the new guests coming in that evening. Mama knew that David—with his new partners in crime, Logan and Reid—would have finished almost all the food that had been brought over from the Davises' refrigerator. Besides, although Mama liked leftovers as much as anyone, after the first day, she wanted fresh food and figured that everyone else did as well.

"I will never understand why people have mold growing on their food in the refrigerator. If you can't eat it the day after, throw it away. The flavor is lost after that!" Mama had chided.

Finley and Whitt had bitten their tongues. Both were known to hold on to certain foods, especially those that were made only on special occasions, for a few days longer than Mama recommended. *That would be a lovely way to off someone,* Whitt had thought. *Poison their leftovers. People would just assume that the reaction to the poison was a reaction to food that had gone bad and would never give it a second thought—until the person failed to wake up in the morning.*

Mama greeted Max and Finley at the side door off the kitchen. "I know I'm pulling you away from your guests, but you need to have something to serve them," she said. Finley was determined to go in, get the provisions, and get out. She didn't want to be waylaid by cousins trying to catch up on five years of life in fifteen minutes. "What time does Mooney get in? And tell me about this new boyfriend of hers!"

Mama was spooning sweet potato souffle into a container, to be served alongside baked macaroni and cheese, green beans, and new potatoes. She had already sliced a tenderloin of beef and slipped the container into the picnic hamper. The platter of fried chicken was almost cooled and ready to be wrapped in paper towels and foil. Max waited patiently, holding the container for the sweet potatoes, while Mama paused midair, spoon in hand, waiting for Finley to give her the lowdown on Ian Bishop.

Ian was Mooney's latest boyfriend, and it looked like this one was serious. She had broken up with her longtime honey, Chris Hartley, a few years ago. He'd been the love of her life, the one everyone thought would be her partner down the aisle. But children had been the difference they could never resolve, and, after much thought, Mooney decided that she wouldn't be happy without kids. She took her time getting back into the dating saddle after her split with Chris. In the time since, she'd had a few relationships, but they'd never lasted long. Until Ian.

"His name is Ian Bishop. He's a trader. I think FX," Finley started to relay, before her mother interrupted her.

"Honey, what is FX?" Mama raised her eyes from covering both the sweet potatoes and a key lime pie with plastic wrap.

"Sorry, Mama. Foreign exchange. He trades dollars into euros or pounds into yen for big companies who have overseas operations," Finley explained. "Anyway, he's from Scarsdale, went to college in Vermont. Middlebury, I think. Fell into banking and has lived in Manhattan since graduation."

"How did they meet?" Mama took the empty sweet potato bowl to the sink and rinsed it, wiping her hands on her apron as she turned to listen to the story.

"He attended a wedding, and she was there as a bridesmaid. She was a friend of the bride, and he was there for the groom," Finley recounted.

"Sounds just like your granny and grandpa. Mom was a bridesmaid and Daddy H. was one of the groomsmen," Mama chuckled. "Daddy H. always joked Mom made him walk down the aisle with her twice."

Mama put the freshly made rolls in the hamper and closed the lid. "I think that does it. Tell your Daddy hello and goodbye. He just pulled into the garage. I know you need to be on your way!"

Max planted a kiss on Mama's cheek before carefully lifting the overfilled hamper off the table. He had gotten used to the "give me some sugar" culture that pervaded Southern houses. He realized he'd fallen into the kissing rhythm of the South when, at some point, someone at Mama and Daddy's house hadn't given him a kiss in greeting or parting. He had asked Finley later if he had somehow offended them.

"No, that line of the family is kind of standoffish," Finley had replied when Max asked after the third person in one group of cousins had given a nod instead of a kiss. "But don't you worry. The mama's side of that family more than makes up for it. You'll see them later tonight. Those are the kissing cousins."

Finley grabbed the grocery bags off the kitchen table—one that held a strawberry dump cake and another that was filled with sauces, gravy, and condiments. She brushed her lips gently against her mother's cheek and headed out the door. When she and Max opened the gate, Daddy was just getting out of the car.

"You off already, sweetheart?"

"Yeah, Daddy. Mama called us over for a food run."

Daddy chortled. "If that woman couldn't find somebody to feed, I think she'd just shrivel up and die. So, please keep eating. I can't do without her!"

Daddy pecked Finley on the head and helped Max settle the food in the trunk before shaking his hand. "You drive carefully now. Wouldn't want your mama to hear that the cakes slid or the pies spilled out!"

Finley climbed into the driver's seat as her daddy closed the door. "Yes, Daddy. I'll drive carefully." She flashed her daddy a big smile. Daddy patted her hand through the open window as she backed the car out of the drive.

At the end of the street, Finley checked her rearview mirror. It had become a habit after an incident in law school when she forgot her notebook in the car and, despite running down the middle of the street waving her arms and calling after her father, who had dropped her off, she'd had to wait until he got to his office to call him. In the hour it took him to return to school with her notes, she vowed that she would always check her rearview regularly, just in case.

As she turned the corner, she noticed a blue sedan slip into traffic. The car followed a couple of cars behind, taking every turn she did, including a couple of shortcuts through the neighborhood to get to the bridge. Once over the bridge, Finley took a right instead of the usual left and headed north.

"Where are we going?" Max asked, seeing the apparent diversion.

"Just looking at a new apartment building they put up on the northside." Finley quickly checked the mirror and, seeing no one behind her, relaxed her shoulders and proceeded to the new construction. "Just curious."

The cluster of new apartments gentrified a section of town that was one of the last to be developed. To build, the developers had had to reclaim the marshes, a thankless task that was sure to fail when the hurricanes came. "Nice view, but you'd have to be on one of the upper floors come the rains," Finley observed as she turned the car south again. Max nodded.

Finley was halfway down Meeting Street, almost to the turn on Wentworth, when she caught sight of the blue car again. The driver had hidden it among some parked cars and pulled out as soon as Finley passed.

"I think we're being followed," Finley remarked, her eyes fixed on the car in her rearview.

"What?" Max started to turn to look behind him but stopped himself. "Why would anyone be following us?"

"I don't know. I tried to divert them, but they waited. They must know where we live, so no point in trying to misdirect them. Just be careful getting out," Finley advised.

Instead of diverting again, Finley drove straight to the Rutledge house and pulled in front, parking behind two police cars that had claimed the prime spots. The blue sedan rolled past them and headed toward the lake, the driver unrecognizable with a baseball cap that covered a good portion of his face. Logan met them at the curb.

"What's going on?" Finley asked as she got out of the car. She took advantage of his presence to pass him food to carry into the house. "You look a little agitated."

"Wanted to give you a heads-up that the police are back. They're searching the house again and reinterviewing your sister and David. She is none too pleased! Just thought I'd warn you."

"What are they looking for this time?" Finley crinkled her brow. She closed the trunk and followed Logan and Max, now laden down with the hamper and food bags, into the house.

"Don't know," Logan mumbled over his shoulder, as he reached the porch and waited for Finley to open the door.

Finley cast a glance into the sunroom as she walked toward the kitchen. The glass door to that room, which was normally thrown open, had been closed. She could just catch a glimpse of Whitt's face through the paned door. Whitt was saying something, hands gesturing, face contorted. *She is not a happy girl! Do they really think she and David know something? What could it be? And do they think another search of the house is going to magically yield something that wasn't there before?*

Finley pointed out to Logan and Max where she wanted the food bags placed on the kitchen counter and then began to unpack all that Mama had sent over. She didn't mention the blue sedan.

"Where're the rest of the crew?" she asked, as she moved food-stuffs around in the refrigerator to make room for the new provisions.

"Reid and Kirsten went to the beach after breakfast this morning and haven't been seen since. Charlie is by the pool with Hema, trying hard to stay out of the way," Logan stated. "I was attempting to work upstairs, but it's hard with people tromping through the house."

Finley looked up briefly. She could hear the heavy footsteps as someone made their way down the upstairs corridor. "How long have they been here?"

"They got here just after you guys left. When I heard them on the porch, I thought initially it was you returning because you had forgotten something." Logan peeked at his watch. "Goodness, that was almost two hours ago!"

"They were searching all that time?" Finley paused in putting away food and stared at Logan. Max continued to lean against the counter, passing her containers from the hamper, but he registered the concern on her face. "And how long have they been with Whitt and David?"

"Almost the whole time," Logan said quietly.

"Well, there's nothing we can do at this stage. Anything we say to try to help is likely to be misconstrued if they're stupid enough to think that either of them had anything to do with this mess," Finley muttered in disgust. "Some wedding week!"

Finley and Max grabbed a glass of Arnold Palmer before following Logan out to the pool deck. *I feel like topping this off with bourbon, but the police would probably have a field day with that!* Finley considered, as she collapsed in the lounge chair Max pulled over for her.

"Greetings!" Hema said to Finley and Max before addressing Logan, her head tilted toward the house. "Are they still there?"

Logan nodded and slid into the chair beside her. He unzipped his pants and slipped them off, revealing a pair of swim trunks underneath. "I was appointed designated watch for you two. I have postponed my swim to alert you to the presence of the constabulary.

Now, having fulfilled my mission, I am more than ready for that swim." The last words were almost drowned out by the cannonball he artfully executed into the deep end of the pool.

"He is such a clown! Even in the face of all this!" Hema shook her head with a half smile. She turned to Finley. "I hope we can get your sister into a good mood once they've left. This is her wedding, for heaven's sake!"

Finley and Charlie nodded in agreement. "We will. Mooney and her new boyfriend are coming in about an hour, so that will distract her. And then we have dinner tonight at Husk, one of her favorite places, so that should put her in a better mood," Finley shared.

From inside, Finley could hear movement and commotion. She got up from her chair and headed back into the house, with Max at her heels. When they came through the kitchen, Whitt was leaning on David, tears drenching her face. David was silent, his hands gently wiping her cheeks.

"Officer Cabot, how nice to see you! I take it you have a suspect, or you wouldn't be here." Finley opined. "So, what's going on?"

From the looks on Whitt's and David's faces, she surmised they were Cabot's prime suspects, but she planned to let him build the logic scaffold that would hang him rather than rush in. She stifled the rising impulse to throttle him. She would kill him with words, in due time.

"He thinks we did it," Whitt blubbered. "He's taking us down to the station for questioning."

"Oh, and what are the grounds on which you are taking them in? Did you find additional evidence in your latest search?" Finley asked in her best prosecutorial voice. Logan, wrapped in a shocking pink beach towel, had come in from outside and stood in the kitchen doorway, listening. Hema and Charlie soon joined him.

Officer Cabot cut a glance at one of his officers, who shook his head sheepishly. "Just as I thought, when I heard your officer give the 'all clear.'" Finley smiled wryly at Cabot. Officer Horton, who she presumed had been leading the search of the rooms, came down the stairs and stood by her partner, stone-faced. Finley continued, "By the way, do you mind if I take a look at your warrant?"

Officer Horton spoke in a firm, directive voice. "Ms. Blake, our questioning has nothing to do with you. I suggest you and the others step back outside."

Finley focused her attention directly on Horton, even as Cabot went to mollify her, clearly knowing where Finley was going with her line of questioning. "Officer Horton, you are in my home, so it has *everything* to do with me. And again, I ask you and your partner for the warrant under which you conducted the search today."

Cabot touched his partner's arm and took command of the conversation. "We don't have a warrant." He confirmed Finley's suspicion.

"And on what basis did you conduct the search? Did my sister, her fiancé, or any of the other guests consent to be searched?" Finley watched as both Horton and Cabot shook their heads. "So, the search you just conducted was illegal?"

Cabot stared at Finley. She didn't blink. Finley continued, "And during the course of this illegal search, did you find any evidence that would support your decision to bring Whitt and David in for additional questioning?"

Cabot again shook his head. Finley responded to this gesture with an additional question. "And during the hour-long interrogation of my sister and her fiancé in the sunroom, did you discover anything additional, or even different, from what was in their original statement?"

Finley glanced over at her sister, who continued sobbing, her face still buried in David's chest. "Oh, by the way, did you at any time read them their rights or advise them that they were under suspicion?"

Horton interjected, "There was no need. They weren't being arrested."

"They weren't being arrested, and yet you were rifling through their belongings—and mine—looking for something with which to implicate them, while you"—Finley snapped around to glare at Cabot—"Officer Cabot, gave them the third degree! And now you want to take them down to the station to put the screws to them again!"

Finley cocked her head to one side as she continued to stare at the officers. She waited, let them sweat, gave them time to think of a way out of the noose they had crafted for themselves. Her breath was measured, her words distinct and carefully enunciated.

"I would suggest that you arrest them now and read them their rights." Whitt gasped and started crying again. Finley lasered an unsmiling stare at Cabot, her voice barely above a whisper, "Or leave and go find the real killer. You aren't going to use my family as an expedient pawn."

For your incompetence. She left the last words unspoken, but Cabot winced, hearing them nonetheless. He had taken a chance—a big chance—hoping to find evidence that would close this case. He knew he had overstepped his authority and come up empty-handed.

The room adopted an embarrassed silence. No one moved. The only sound was Whitt's muffled sobs and the birds chirping outside the sunroom windows.

After a few moments, Cabot nodded toward the door, and the two officers who had conducted the upstairs search slipped out the front and down the stairs to their car. Cabot started to speak, but Finley cut him off.

"Should you wish to return with a warrant for yet another search or talk to any of us further, officers, we will be here until at least the day after the wedding. If you wish to detain our guests after that, I recommend you have a damn good reason and the legal basis to do it!"

Cabot nodded and moved toward the door, holding it open for his partner. Horton walked onto the porch but turned to look at Finley as Cabot pulled the door closed. Finley returned her stony stare with a steely one of her own. *Let's see who blinks first when you get back to the station and your captain reads you both the riot act after I call to inform him. You knew you violated protocol and the law as well. You just thought you could get away with it. What else have you been getting away with?*

12

N O SOONER HAD THE POLICE cars pulled away from the curb than Mooney's cab pulled up. Logan saw the taxi approach from the window and ran out, towel flapping, to usher them in.

"Welcome to Charleston!" Logan bellowed, before lowering his voice to a whisper. "Hope you had a restful trip. You're going to need it with all the mayhem here!"

Mooney, in her excitement to greet Logan and introduce Ian, only heard Logan's salutation. She took in Logan's ultracasual attire and laughed. She allowed Logan and Ian to handle paying the taxi and carrying the bags. As she waited, she stood at the bottom of the walkway, admiring the house and grounds.

"This house is simply spectacular. All the houses on this street are," Mooney enthused. "I've been to Charleston before but never have I seen it so pretty. Just for Whitt's wedding!"

Logan came up behind her. "Wait until you see the inside!"

Inside the house, the group that had witnessed Finley's exchange with the police had started to disperse. Hema and Charlie had returned poolside, while Finley and David attended to Whitt.

"David, why don't you take Whitt upstairs so she can wash her face and get settled before Mooney comes in?" Finley had suggested when Logan ran outside to collect Mooney and Ian. When the downstairs cleared, Max gathered Finley in his arms and held her until she exhaled.

"You were brilliant, by the way," Max whispered, then he laughed. "Remind me never to cross you."

"Well, there you are!" Finley cried, pulling away from Max and hugging her friend hard as she walked in. "I thought you had gotten lost! So glad to see you!"

She then turned to greet the man who stood beside Mooney, his hand resting on the small of her back. "Ian, welcome. So glad to finally meet you!"

Mooney stepped in to give Max a kiss in greeting after Finley and Ian had embraced. "And this is Max. Max, Ian." The two men shook hands and politely sized each other up. Max's eyebrow arched slightly in the appraisal.

Ian was of average height, but he still looked tall against Mooney's petiteness. His dark-brown hair was cut short and swept back off his broad brow. His athletic build matched Mooney's runner's muscles.

What struck Finley most profoundly, in looking at him standing next to Max, was his placidity contrasted with Max's intensity. Ian possessed an inner calmness that claimed his eyes and his bearing. Finley chuckled to herself. His eyes reminded her of a sweet cocker spaniel's—dark pools of kindness that made you let down your guard and trust that you were safe in his presence.

"Were those police cars we saw leaving when we pulled up?" Mooney looked directly at Finley. "What are you guys up to now?"

"We'll fill you in over dinner." Logan hurriedly brushed over the question as he led the twosome up the stairs. "I'll show you to your room and then give you a quick tour before I hop in the shower. I think we have a seven-thirty dinner reservation."

Finley confirmed the time for dinner, saying, "We can head out at seven. It's only a fifteen-minute walk from here, and we can take our time."

Finley was thinking of Kirsten, who had just returned from the beach, slightly pink with sunburn, but excited to tell Whitt and the others about her day—after a relaxing soak, of course. Reid had gone to run her bath, knowing that Kirsten would be a little unsteady on her feet with her extra baby load and the low spigots on the bathtub.

While the others got dressed for dinner, Finley went to check on her sister. It had been a trying day, the capper to a week of bizarre and unexpected events that would have unnerved anyone but were especially upsetting to a prospective—and tentative—bride. Finley knocked lightly on the door. David answered, dressed and ready for dinner.

"She's almost ready. Why don't you head on in, and I'll wait downstairs," David said. Finley reached up to give her future brother-in-law a kiss in thanks before slipping into the master bedroom.

Whitt was in the bathroom, applying mascara. She lifted her gaze from her eyelashes to her sister. "Thanks for coming to our rescue. The thought of having to go down to the station, in a police car, was just a little more than I could swallow. Goodness, if Mama had found out, she would have been mortified!"

Finley waved it off. "How are you feeling?"

"Spent, but better now that I don't have to spend the evening at the police station, possibly in a cell."

"Cabot knew better than to try that. All you had to do was use your one call to contact Daddy, or heaven forbid Mama, and all hell would've broken loose. And he knew it," Finley chuckled. "I really doubt he would have even taken you down to the station. He knew he was skating on thin ice."

"He needs to head to church tonight for what he did to us." Whitt was angry now that the fear had passed. "As Granny used to say, 'God don't like ugly.' And both he and Horton had ugly all over them."

"Did they say what they were looking for?"

"The keys. They still haven't found Tommy's keys. They're speculating that they are somewhere among the killer's things."

"Their logic about the keys makes sense. But they already checked the house, inside and out. So why check all of our things—most of which weren't even in the house at the time of the murder? They never would have gotten a warrant for that broad a search, if they could have gotten one at all." Finley joined her sister in the bathroom and started twisting her hair up, getting it ready for her run upstairs for a quick shower before dinner. "So, unless they were thinking of planting something—which would have served no purpose because the keys wouldn't have fit the car—the search was useless."

Whitt sprayed on a spritz of perfume and looked at Finley in the mirror. "To tell you the truth, at this stage, I don't know and don't really care. As long as they leave us alone until after the wedding!"

"And then you can claim the spousal waiver—you can't be compelled to testify against your husband!"

"But he didn't do anything wrong!" Whitt exclaimed, her eyes and mouth hanging open in disbelief at Finley's seeming accusation.

Finley kissed her sister's cheek as she headed for the door, stealing David's signature expression in reply. "I know, sister mine. Calm down. It's all good!"

When the others headed out for Magnolia Plantation shortly after breakfast the next day, Finley and Max headed over to Sullivan's to help Mama with some last-minute wedding preparations. Poor Ian got a good taste of the Blake sister madness over dinner the night before. Husk had had the foresight to give them a large table toward the back of the main room. There, they feasted on the best of local farm-to-table Southern fare. From red corn bourbon to catfish, field peas, and chess pie, the crew tasted the best of the South.

Finley and Whitt wished that they had recorded Ian, Logan, and Hema's reactions to Kirsten's hilarious explanations of Southern traditions and food origins. The best was their attempt to understand mountain oysters. Hema's head almost met her shoulder and her eyes almost crossed as Kirsten and Whitt took turns detailing how the delicacy was harvested. Hema turned to Logan to be sure that she wasn't being punked, but his expression suggested that he knew no more than she did.

The Four Musketeers didn't get around to telling the others about the bones in the attic. An opening in the conversation for that revelation never appeared, so they tacitly agreed to keep silent about it as the others each took turns sharing their accounts of the day.

It didn't take much for the wine, peanut butter pie, and strawberry cake they shared for dessert to lull everyone into a deep food-induced slumber that most were still working through the next morning when Finley and Max started the first pot of coffee. Before long, the aroma had roused the others and plans for the day were confirmed. Finley and Max would take Mama duty—the beginning of their week-long attempt to keep Whitt distracted and Mama occupied. Kirsten would enlist Whitt to help her direct the tour of several plantation houses and gardens just outside Charleston proper.

Finley and Max volunteered to clear up the breakfast dishes so the group could beat the heat with a morning tour.

"Is this a tactical mission or something more strategic?" Max asked as he stacked the dishwasher. Finley glanced at him quickly and smiled at his methodical arrangement of the glasses and silverware in the dishwasher trays.

"You talking about the trip to Mama's?" Finley asked, as she gave the counters and refrigerator a final wipe down before dropping the dishcloth in the dishwasher, too, and turning it on. "I guess you would call it strategic, since there is nothing in particular that we're going to do. Just general help so Daddy doesn't have to carry the full burden of keeping Mama from running off the tracks."

"Is she starting to get worried?" Max leaned on the counter, watching Finley set the kitchen to rights so they could make the trip across the bridge. "She seemed surprisingly calm yesterday, given all that happened."

"She did. But that was yesterday. Daddy said things started to unravel last night. Mama and Albertine got into a difference of opinion. He said he would explain it when we get there."

She leaned into Max as she passed him, taking his hands from the counter and placing them on her waist. He obliged her by tightening the embrace. He gave her a sly smile before lowering his head in the bend of her neck and proceeding to kiss his way to her lips. He lingered there for a moment, his lips barely touching hers, his indescribably delicious eyes dancing across the planes of her face before he committed to a thorough kiss that had her almost limp in his arms at the finish.

"I wasn't expecting that, but I do like surprises! Especially when they come wrapped in your arms." Finley panted, struggling to catch her breath. She straightened up and inhaled deeply. "As much as I would like for you to do that again, we need to go. Daddy will be looking for us!"

Max pecked her lips and released her. He reached into the fridge and pulled out a bottle of water. "Want one?" He held up a bottle.

"My canteen should be in there," Finley replied, just as Max pulled her water bottle out and passed it to her. "Thanks. *Allons-y!*"

Daddy was in the backyard with Daisy when Max and Finley got to the house. Finley had let Max drive now that he knew his way around, so she was free to text her father to see what was happening before she and Max arrived. Daddy had said to meet him around back.

"Hey, sweetheart, how're you today?" Daddy met her with a warm hug. He then shook Max's hand and led them to some chairs at the far end of the pool. There was a small cluster of people closer to the house, talking, with cups of coffee in their hand and what looked like sticky buns on paper plates.

"Mama feeding folks again?" Finley inclined her head toward the coffee crowd.

"And she has been joined by Julie and Peggy." Daddy shook his head. "They took a break, but now they are back in full force. You should see that kitchen! I think every pot and pan has been pulled out. I gave up asking how I could help and just came outside!"

"Should I go do dishes, then?" Finley considered. "Max can keep you company—or he can dry."

Daddy cast a glance at Max. "I think Finley's just volunteered you for KP duty."

"I don't mind." Max rose to indicate his willingness to help. "It'll make the work go faster. Or so they say!"

Finley followed his lead and started into the house before stopping and turning back. "You forgot to tell me what had Mama so exercised."

"Oh. Something about why Albertine went away. I don't understand it and chose to stay out of it. Luckily, there was only me, your mama, and Albertine in the kitchen at the time. I just left and let them talk it out."

"And did they? Talk it out, I mean?" Finley saw her father press his lips together, which generally meant that what was said was not what really was.

"Your mama said it was water under the bridge, but I don't think so. See what you can find out, sweetie. Maybe just letting her talk about whatever was said will take the sting out of whatever's the matter."

Finley bent down and kissed her daddy's head. "I'll see what I can do. See you in a bit, Daddy."

The kitchen wasn't quite as bad as Daddy had described, but he wasn't that far off. Finley wasn't sure what the three sisters were cooking or planned to cook, but Julie was back at the counter measuring out what looked like flour and sugar for some sort of cake, while Peggy and Odessa were chopping onions and celery.

"What are you making?" Finley called out to no one in particular, as she and Max walked in.

Mama looked up from rinsing off the mound of dishes that had accumulated in the sink to smile at her daughter. "Finley, Max, you're up early! I didn't think you would be over until later in the day. Where are Whitt and the others?"

"They headed to Magnolia with Mooney and all for a tour." Finley picked up a raw green bean from the large aluminum soup pot on the table and crunched into it. Max's contorted expression told her that eating raw string beans from the pot before they were cooked hadn't been on his list of favorite childhood memories. "We came to relieve you of kitchen duty. Move over."

Finley used her hip to bump her mother from her place in front of the sink. Mama stripped off her apron and tied it around Finley before passing a dish towel to Max. "Gladly. Now I can enjoy another cup of coffee."

While Finley rinsed, Max stacked all the dishes that would fit into the dishwasher and then turned to drying as Finley started washing the remaining dishes by hand. As they worked, they listened to her mama and aunts list all the dishes they were making for dinner that evening.

"Julie's making another bourbon cake. The last one barely survived an hour before being reduced to crumbs. Bubba, Aunt Mayree's boy, almost finished half of it off himself!" Mama shook her head in amazement. "David's parents got in late last night. Their flight was delayed. They're sleeping in, according to Cora. Peggy and Odessa are chopping for the dressing. Turkey's already in. Will you be joining us for dinner?"

"Nope. We have a ghost tour tonight that starts at dusk." Finley folded the dishcloth and laid it on the sink edge when the last of the dishes were cleaned. "Any of y'all want to come?"

"No siree, Bob!" Odessa cried, her eyes wide. "I have no need whatsoever for ghosts. They leave me alone, and I leave them alone."

Max had to chuckle at Odessa's adamance. He was of the same mind but was being a good sport in agreeing to accompany the rest of the group later that evening. He knew that Finley wasn't too keen on the outing either, but she had positioned it as an opportunity to learn more about Charleston's history.

Mama got up from the kitchen table and poured herself more coffee. "Can I interest you two in a cup?" She held the pot up in offer.

Finley nodded and pulled a cup from the sideboard. Max declined, heading for the side door that led to the backyard. "If my duties are concluded here, I think I'll sit out back with your father and Daisy."

"In that case, Finley, why don't we head onto the porch so I can put my feet up for a quick spell?" Mama asked, then she turned to her sisters and Odessa. "You girls'll be okay for a few minutes?"

Mama waited for the other women's replies before leading Finley through the dining room toward the front of the house. The front porch connected to a small screened side veranda that was decorated with white wicker benches and caned armchairs. It was there that Mama headed. When she reached one of the armchairs, she collapsed into it and kicked off her shoes before resting her feet in the opposite chair.

"Goodness, I'm tired. I'm getting too old for this." Mama sighed deeply. "I'm secretly glad that you and Max took the easy way out and didn't want a big wedding."

Mama had been surprisingly accommodating about Max and Finley's "committed permanence without marriage" arrangement. All Mama had asked was whether the two were truly devoted to each other, which they were. Beyond that, she and Daddy had said nothing. It was with that blessing that Max and Finley had started their lives together, almost a year earlier.

Mama looked over at Finley, who had taken a seat on the cushioned bench, her coffee resting in her lap. "You two haven't changed your minds on that, have you?"

Her question took on a certain urgent tone as she studied her daughter's face. Finley caught the undercurrent of panic in her mother's query. She was almost tempted to tease her mama and say that Whitt's wedding had given Max and her second thoughts about their casual arrangement. She decided Mama looked too exhausted just now for mind games.

"No, Mama," Finley laughed. "We're fine as is. But you look completely tuckered out. Why are you cooking so much?"

Mama exhaled heavily before taking a sip of her coffee. "It's not the cooking and preparations that are weighing on me. It's just everything else."

"Tommy and the bones at the Beaufort house?" Finley reached to touch her mama's hand.

"No. Although that is indeed unsettling. Murder seems to follow you girls wherever you go, like a bad penny." Mama eyed Finley sternly before softening her voice. "No, family matters."

"Something about Albertine?" Finley hurried on after her mama gave her mention of Albertine a startled look. "Daddy told me that you and Albertine had words. You want to talk about it?"

Mama slowly sipped her coffee, pondering. After several moments, she put her cup on the side table and directed her gaze at Finley. "Albertine has been blackmailing her ex-husband."

13

"SAY WHAT?" FINLEY BLURTED OUT before she could catch herself. Mama never liked to share family secrets too freely. She said it made family business common, like grocery store gossip, instead of cherished and closely held, as she thought it should be. But Mama had dropped the blackmail bomb and it needed some clarification. "Walk it back a little, Mama, and fill me in on the details. I just met these people."

Mama adjusted herself in the chair to face Finley more directly. "Albertine had a bit too much bourbon last night, and, after the others left the kitchen, she started talking out of her head. It was just me and your daddy. After a little while, your daddy headed out back."

Mama continued. "That's when she poured herself another bourbon and really started talking freely. Perhaps too freely.

"She said that leaving her husband, Buster, was the best thing that happened to her. Now, mind you, how she left. She just walked off in the middle of the night. Said she was going to get more milk and never came back. Left Buster and Lael, who was in high school, in Port Royal. Just like that. Next thing we know, she is in Chicago. Sent a note to her sister, who was in North Charleston at the time, as if that was enough.

"So, last night, she started talking about how she was able to make some money once she was in Chicago. And then, she started giggling." Mama adopted Albertine's high-pitched, slow-crawl of voice, "'And then I made a little more off that no-good husband of mine,' she says. So, I asked what she meant by that. It turns out that she and Buster never divorced after Albertine left, so when he married again, he was a bigamist. And Albertine blackmailed him over it. He was a pastor in the church. It would have ruined him."

Finley's mouth dropped open. She had heard a fair share of family gossip—poor choices made by relatives that had cost jobs, marriages, custody of children. But to date, as least as far back as she could remember, there had never been anything like blackmail or bigamy that skirted the law so blatantly.

Mama gulped down the last of her coffee. "Needless to say, I was incensed. That hussy had just walked off and left her child to fend for herself. She should have had the decency to divorce Buster, at the very least, not blackmail him. Let the law handle it if he was doing something that was grounds for divorce or prosecution!

"Poor Lael never really recovered. She stayed with Tommy's family until graduation and then left for college. Her mama didn't want her, and after her daddy got remarried—less than a year after Albertine left—he didn't want her either, so Lael was just left with Tommy's mama, Albertine's sister."

Mama pulled her legs off the chair and stood up. She picked up her cup and reached for Finley's. "Last night, I let her have it. I just couldn't believe her being so cavalier about what she'd done to her child. It was a silly little game to her. She had put one over on Buster! To hell with all the others whose lives she had disrupted."

At that, Mama opened the porch door and headed back to the kitchen, leaving Finley to try to make sense of the deluge of truths that Mama had just rained down on her. Now Finley understood why Lael and Tommy had hung out together all those years ago. They had grown up together. *Doesn't excuse their evil*, Finley thought, *but it does explain their closeness.*

Finley sat on the sunporch for several minutes. Her ruminations kept tying tenuous little threads between Albertine, Buster, Tommy, and Lael. Every time she tried to knot a thread to hold a connection fast, the logic would unravel, and the thread slip through. *These people are connected and so are the murders. It's too coincidental for the same family to discover two bodies within a week of each other. God doesn't believe in coincidence, and neither do I*, Finley pondered. *I just have to find and resolve the connection.*

Finley didn't bother going back inside. She unlatched the screen door and followed the graveled path that led from the side of the house to the backyard. Max, Daddy, and Daisy were in the same place she had left Daddy and Daisy an hour earlier. Max and Daddy both had mugs, but she doubted that the only thing in them was coffee. It was creeping to noon on a lazy Southern afternoon. That called for adding fortification to the morning brew.

When she neared where Max and Daddy were sitting, Daisy broke free to greet her.

"Are you keeping these boys out of trouble, Miss Daisy?" Finley ruffled her neck and then her belly. She could see from the heaviness of Max's eyelids that her supposition about the bourbon-coffee concoction hadn't been far off. "What are you guys up to?"

Daddy, figuring he had been found out, fessed up. "Just enjoying a nice Southern spring in the good ol' boys' way. Your man here can hold his own."

"How many have you had?" Finley stared incredulously at the drinking game that had started early. She wondered whether it was her daddy just being friendly or whether he was still testing the man she'd "married." Either way, neither Daddy nor Max was drunk, but they were feeling little pain. "Shall I get you something to absorb the alcohol?"

"Nah, girl, we haven't had much. Just a couple cups of coffee. Odessa brought the pot out. I think she was trying to sweeten up your guy because she then brought out the flask!"

Max's smile was lopsided. "It seemed impolite to say no."

"You two are incorrigible! I thought the two of you couldn't get into much mess out here. Boy, was I wrong!"

"Wrong about what?" Mama had crept up behind her. She was looking back and forth between Daddy and Max. "Ry, did you get that poor boy plastered? And before noon, no less!"

"Nooo, Kitty Kat. He isn't drunk, and neither am I. We can handle it. Besides, we aren't going anywhere, so what does it matter?"

"Well, you certainly aren't now! I was going to ask you to run down to Savannah and pick up Aunt Lavinia. Her housekeeper was supposed to drive her up later today for the wedding, but the poor girl has a stomach bug and doesn't want to risk it. So, Aunt Vinnie called to say she couldn't make it. I told her nonsense, but I may have spoken too quickly."

Aunt Lavinia was Mama's grandaunt, somehow or other. Perhaps through marriage. In any event, she was a beloved octogenarian who racked up regular attendance at family weddings and funerals. A wedding without Aunt Vinnie just wouldn't be the same.

"We can go get her, Mama," Finley piped up. "I'll drive, of course, but Max can ride shotgun and sleep it off."

Max took his chastisement silently and good-naturedly. His blue eyes deepened in color under the hood of his drowsy lids, and the crookedness of his smile grew more pronounced. "Whatever you say, sweetheart. Whither thou goest, I go."

"Don't start quoting poetry to escape. You aren't out of the doghouse yet. And don't even think of getting David drunk before the wedding. Mama *will* kill you!" Finley shifted her gaze to laser in on Max. "As best man, Mama—and I—will hold you directly responsible if he is not here on Saturday in top form for the wedding. Any alley catting you boys plan to do as a bachelor party needs to be done tomorrow night so he can have time to sober up!"

"Yes, ma'am. As you say," Max intoned and stood up. "Do I have time to run to the washroom before we head out to get your aunt?"

Finley nodded as Max headed into the pool house to find the facilities.

"Don't be too hard on him. I was egging him on. He rose to the occasion and held his own. I'm impressed," Daddy chuckled. "My girls found good men I feel proud to call family."

Finley bent down and planted a kiss on her daddy's cheek. "Just don't drown them in liquor before they are fully seasoned. Whitt and I are rather fond of them."

Mama shook her head and chuckled. "I'll call Aunt Vinnie and let her know you're coming to get her. I won't tell her why Ry can't make it!"

Daddy grabbed Mama's hand and pulled her into his lap. "Don't get on me too bad, woman! It's been a long time since I've gotten whizzed midday. Cut me a little slack!"

Mama leaned back to take a good look at the handsome bear on whose lap she sat. It was true that lapses like this were rare for Ry. She was glad that he felt close enough to Max to tease him like this. There was a time, after Finley had returned to the US from Morocco, that the mention of the man's name had set him on edge. To Daddy, Max was the man who broke his darling girl's heart. Time and Finley's enduring love for the man had softened his stance. By all accounts, it seemed that her husband understood now what Finley saw in him.

Aunt Vinnie was ready and waiting for Finley and Max when they pulled up in front of her house, a compact brick ranch with a low stone fence. A younger cousin had stood in for her sick housekeeper, fixing the old woman's hair and making sure that everything she wanted was in her suitcase and pocketbook. Before Finley and Max reached the door, it was flung open, and Aunt

Vinnie was striding toward the car, her cousin pulling a travel bag behind her.

"Nan, did you pack a shawl for me, dear?" Aunt Vinnie smiled at her request for a wrap in eighty-degree weather. "I know you think it's warm but, at my age, every day comes with a chill!"

The young woman, tall and reed thin with a mass of curly brown hair, assured her that there were at least two shawls in the bag, an everyday one and another for the wedding. Nan reminded her that she had another draped over her shoulders. She also confirmed that they had walked through the house twice already, making sure everything was out of the plugs, the gas was turned off, and all the lights, except those on the timer, were flicked off.

"You have a good time, Auntie. I'll lock up and hold your key until you get back," Finley's young cousin called out as Max helped the older woman into the car. "And bring me back a piece of wedding cake for under my pillow!"

Max climbed in the back to quietly sleep off the effects of the morning's fortified coffee, but sleep was not easily found. Finley's aunt peppered him with questions about his background, his family, his work, and all the places he'd been. Finley caught his eye in the rearview mirror as he politely responded to her queries. When the first round had been exhausted, Aunt Vinnie returned to a few of the locations and began to probe deeper.

"Do you think the Arab Spring will cause real change in the status of women in the Middle East?" Aunt Vinnie asked.

Finley had to pause. She chided herself for thinking that the old woman's topics of conversation would be limited to recipes and garden tips. Mama had said that Aunt Vinnie and her husband had loved to travel. Although Canada was as far outside the US as they had been able to go, they were well-read and, as it appeared, curious about the world.

Finley shared her opinion on the Arab Spring before Max gave his. Max followed his response with a few questions to Aunt Vinnie about her experience as a woman in a gender-biased world. For almost an hour, the trio debated issues of foreign policy and probed domestic challenges. In between, Aunt Vinnie gave them updates on her cats, a Persian called Isis and a Russian Blue named Boris.

When they passed the exit sign for Beaufort on the highway, Aunt Vinnie shifted the conversation. "Your mama got Charlotte and Harland's little house in Beaufort, didn't she?" Aunt Vinnie asked. "When they moved to Sullivan's, they had a nice group of renters in the place. Some nice families. Charlotte and I would keep up with each other, even when we couldn't see each other."

She didn't wait for a response before continuing on. "I haven't been to the Beaufort house in years. As I recall, that Hale boy from Edisto was renting it from your Mama and Daddy. Seems a nice enough boy. Albertine shouldn't have run off on him like that."

Finley jolted slightly at the mention of Albertine's name. She was confused. Who was she saying Albertine had run off on? She hadn't heard the name Hale associated with Albertine before. Only Buster. She assumed that was a first name or nickname. The only surname used with Albertine and Lael was Garrett.

"I really don't know who was renting it lately. I think Daddy and Mama have had the same renter in the house since Mama inherited it. Almost five years now," Finley stated.

"Yes, that would be the Hale boy. He moved in there from Port Royal with his second wife. As I heard it, he and this new woman lived in the Port Royal place after Albertine ran off. They stayed there almost ten years before they moved out here. Think this place was closer to his new church."

Finley could see Max's head lolling back every now and then. She wished she could get him to wake up and listen more closely to what Aunt Vinnie was saying. Maybe this was the connective tissue between Albertine, Buster, Lael, and Tommy that she had been missing. She would have to remember as much as she could and then talk it through with Whitt when she came back from the plantation tour. The logical person to review the facts with would have been Mama, since she knew family history that might be relevant. But

Finley had a better chance of winning the Nobel Peace Prize than she did getting her Mama to help them solve these two murders.

Finley caught the tail end of Aunt Vinnie's last comment. It was enough to draw her immediately back into the conversation.

". . . haven't heard mention of him, or his wife—the second one—in a long while," Aunt Vinnie remarked.

"I'm sorry, Aunt Vinnie. I got distracted. What was that you just said?" Finley interjected.

"I was just saying that I haven't heard mention of either him or his wife in a year or so. The wife longer—she may have left him, too. You never know with young people today. Just never know."

Finley looked back to see Max sitting upright now, his brow knitted as he considered what Aunt Vinnie just said. *He's thinking the same thing I am—that body in the Beaufort house is known to us. This involves family!*

A glance toward the passenger seat revealed that further questioning was not an option. Aunt Vinnie had nodded off to sleep.

By the time they had dropped Aunt Vinnie off at Aunt Cora and Uncle John's house and started back over the bridge to the Rutledge house, it was after five. The ghost tour of Charleston was to start at six thirty, and Finley wanted a shower to rinse off the road dirt.

"Pretty interesting stuff Aunt Vinnie was saying about the people who lived in the Beaufort house, eh?" Finley asked, after Max moved back into the passenger seat and got settled for the ride across the bridge.

"Yeah, I didn't catch all of it but enough to start thinking that your parents' tenant might know who those bones belong to," Max suggested. "But it still doesn't answer where the tenant himself is? He hasn't surfaced yet, despite having several people looking for him."

"That's true. But I suspect if we find him, a lot of these questions will be answered."

Finley and Max had just walked in the door when Finley's cell rang. It was Daddy.

"Hey, girl. Can you and your sister hop on the phone and your computer real quick? I know you guys are going out, but the Beaufort police just called and asked that we join them on a call to look at some pictures of the things that were in the attic. They're hoping you might recognize something." Daddy paused to steady his voice. "I told them, once again, that it was unlikely we would recognize any of this stuff, but they asked that we get on the call to confirm."

Finley could tell Daddy was starting to get a bit exasperated, but she knew it wouldn't do to not cooperate with the officers.

"Hold on. Let me call Whitt in, and we can get on now." While Finley summoned Whitt, she advised Max to go get dressed so the bathroom would be clear when she headed up. With Whitt beside her, Finley pulled up her computer and put the phone on speaker.

"Okay. Daddy, go ahead and patch them in," Finley told him.

The two officers who had handled the investigation at the Beaufort house earlier came on the phone. "Evening, Misses Blake, General, Mrs. Blake. Sorry to bother you, but we are trying to find any leads so that we can identify the bones, understand the source of the money, and contact the tenant you had in the house."

"Sorry to interrupt, Officer, but who do you have down as tenant in the house?" Finley inquired.

"Mr. Elijah Hale."

"Two questions: what was his previous known address, and do you know if he went by any other names?" Finley asked.

"Miss Blake, we normally ask the questions. Do you have further information in this case? If so, you need to come forward with it."

Finley could see the bafflement on Whitt's face and hear her mama questioning her father in the background. "I may. I went to pick up my great-aunt a couple hours ago, and she said some things that may be relevant."

"Such as, ma'am?"

"Such as that the person renting the house, the Mr. Hale, may have been a cousin from Edisto. That he and his second wife moved from Port Royal into the house. That after about a year, they stopped seeing the wife. They figured she'd run off like the man's first wife did. And that they haven't seen or heard from the man in a few months, which corresponds to the time when he stopped paying rent. The bigger revelation for me was that Mr. Hale and my cousin's ex-husband, Buster, may be one in the same person."

Finley followed up with a question to Mama. "Mama, do you know Buster's last name?"

Mama's response was quick. "No. Just Buster. I had no reason to know it. I never had much dealing with him. Garrett is Albertine's—the first wife and my cousin—maiden name. She never changed it. If that's the case, I don't know why Lael—that's her daughter—switched to using Garrett instead of Hale."

One of the officer's cleared his throat. "This is helpful information. Maybe your cousin knows where we can find her ex-husband."

Mama sighed. "I doubt it. But Lael may know where to find her daddy. Strange that she would rent the house to her father and stepmama and never say that was who our tenants were. Not that it would have mattered to me or your daddy, but it just seems strange."

The officer cleared his throat again. "I agree that all of this will need to be checked out. Can you give us the name and address of your cousin and her daughter so that we can contact them? Also, it might help to talk to your great-aunt, if that wouldn't be too much of a bother for her?" He continued, "And while we are gathering that, we sent over some pictures of the evidence that was collected from the house. Can you please look over them and let us know if anything looks familiar?"

Whitt used the touchpad to open the file that had been sent over. The first few frames of the bones, taken outside of the bag now and laid in some semblance of skeletal order, and of the ziplocked bags of money, elicited no response. However, when they reached the fifth frame, a shot of a garbage bag split open and several smaller pouches peeking out from under a few more ziplocked bags, Whitt and Finley both leaned forward. Finley adjusted the settings to enlarge the grainy image.

"The little piece of cloth that's sticking out from under the money bags. Both my sister and I think we've seen it before, but we can't be sure. And we are drawing a blank on where we saw it, if indeed we did," Whitt offered. "Not much help. Sorry. Maybe it will come to us later."

The officer sighed. "If it comes to you later, please let us know. Anything will be helpful. This has already given us some leads we can follow. Again, sorry to bother you, but we are looking at anything and everything to identify the bones and to find Mr. Hale. Thanks again for your cooperation."

No sooner had the police and her parents clicked off than it dawned on Finley whose bag the pouch resembled. "Lael!"

14

WHITT REFRESHED THE IMAGE ON the computer screen and scrolled through the pictures again. When she reached the fifth frame, she stopped. "You're right! It's the same as Lael's satchel."

The corner of a Victorian floral pattern in pinks, greens, and grays came into focus. Based on what little was visible, it was unclear whether the pattern was part of a bag, portfolio, or wallet.

"It's hers," Finley whispered. "She said there had been a couple pouches, but she didn't know where they had gone."

"Do you think she killed that woman? Her daddy's second wife?" Whitt asked. "Got angry with her for taking her daddy away and did her in?"

"But why wait so long? If Aunt Vinnie's timeline is right, Lael would have waited for ten years!"

"Ten years for what?" Logan and Hema had ambled down the stairs, dressed for the ghost walk, and caught the last part of the conversation.

"To murder her stepmama," Whitt explained matter-of-factly. Hema stepped back behind Logan and held onto his arm for additional protection.

"Why would she kill her stepmother? Who are these people?" Hema's voice trembled slightly.

"It's complicated, but we can try to explain what we think we know while we're heading to the ghost walk. Let me just go get dressed real quick." Finley was already halfway up the stairs.

While Finley showered and dressed, Logan reminded Hema of the Blake sisters' strange law of attraction to murder. Hema had seen it in Jaipur, so she knew firsthand how the sisters discovered murder wherever they went. When Finley and Max came downstairs to join them, the rest of the crew was huddled around Logan as he recounted the strange events during their adventure in Jaipur, with the bejeweled dowagers who ended up planted around the hotel gardens.

"We'd better go before Logan convinces everyone that Whitt and I are murder magnets," Finley announced. "We can walk. It's only a couple of blocks."

"Do you think it's safe?" Hema quietly inquired.

Finley approached her and put an arm around her friend. "It's perfectly safe. The bones we found in Beaufort were from several years ago, and the police are investigating the money. Besides, it was at a completely different house and may have nothing to do with the body that was found here."

Max sidled up behind Finley and whispered in her ear, "If that was supposed to make her feel better, I don't think it was effective."

Finley stepped back to look at Hema's face. The poor woman's eyes had widened unnaturally so that her lovely almond-shaped orbs looked like fried eggs, the irises completely surrounded by the whites and plopped into expanded sockets. Her mouth matched her eyes, frozen into a perfectly rounded O. The veins in her neck had swum to the surface and painted tiny, bluish-green swim lanes under the skin.

Finley nodded forlornly to Max as she headed for the door. "Hema, guys, we need to go. There are some developments yesterday that we haven't had a chance to fill you in on. But we will when we have a chance to sit down. For now, let's just enjoy our walking Charleston history lesson."

The ghost tour took the group through parts of the French Quarter that Whitt and Finley had never heard of. The group wandered into church cemeteries, the old slave market, and haunted mansions. But then the guide, a college student named Luke who was majoring in Southern colonial history, took them into the Provost Dungeon, where patriots during the Revolutionary War met their demise. The whistle of the wind through the narrow, vaulted brick passages sounded so much like whispers that Hema and Whitt almost climbed into Logan's and David's arms at one point. The tour of the old city jail, which had housed pirates, prostitutes, and murderers, had Kirsten in stitches, laughing over a story about John and Lavinia Fisher, hoteliers from the 1800s who poisoned their guests.

"Well, at least we haven't been done in by the housekeeper at our house," Kirsten observed. "Although, we have no idea what your mother and her sisters have been baking into those cakes and brownies."

"If there had been anything poisonous in them, David would be dead by now!" Whitt teased, taking her fiancé's hand. "I think we're all safe."

By the time they sauntered into the Blind Tiger Pub after the tour ended, they were ready for food and libations. Murder had pervaded their every thought for almost two hours. While they had joked about the sordid and macabre details of the accidents, hangings, and killings that Luke recounted during the ghost tour, the real body and bones found in the houses they were living in haunted them more vividly.

The waitress had just brought their drinks when Hema could hold back no longer. "Maybe no one else is wondering, but I need to know what it is that you have not told us about another body that you found."

"Actually, it's just bones." Finley glanced over at her sister.

Taking her cue, Whitt began the tale of the body in the attic. Periodically, David or Max would add a fact or comment. Finley watched as Whitt enthralled them with a story woven from what was known at the time and what had been learned since.

"So that leaves us with several questions," Finley said, after Whitt ended her saga and the food was served. "First, who was the person that is now the bones? Second, where is Mr. Hale? Third, are he and Lael's daddy one and the same? Fourth, where did all that money come from and is that the reason for the bones? And finally, are these bones connected to the body Whitt and David found?"

Finley turned to look at Whitt before offering David and Max the floor. "Am I missing anything?"

The group was silent for several minutes. No one, not even David, touched their food. Even the babies in utero paused their kicking for a moment to consider the questions before them. After a while, Charlie broke the silence.

"How do you guys get into these situations?" Charlie's puzzled gaze jumped between Whitt and Finley.

"Don't look at us!" Whitt exclaimed. "We don't go looking for bodies. They just show up. Unexpected and definitely uninvited!"

"That said, we have less than two days to solve this thing." Finley stared at her sister defiantly as she took a sip of her Sauvignon Blanc. "I refuse to have you walking down the aisle with this hanging over your head. If it's family related, you could have the very murderer sitting at your backyard wedding."

"Another reason for us to get there early so we can sit close to the front. Killers like to hang toward the back," Logan shared with a grin. "At least, they do in the movies."

Finley laughed at Logan's observation. "The other information we just discovered is that Lael may somehow be connected to the money."

"Why do you say that?" Logan asked. "I didn't particularly like her on the occasions I've been around her, but she doesn't look like the type who would bother getting her hands dirty with anything illegal."

Whitt finished the bite of pub burger in her mouth. "Lael had a satchel made of the same patterned material that we saw in one of the police photos. She said the satchel had a smaller companion pouch that she lost. And then, all of a sudden, it shows up in an attic full of ill-gotten money and human bones?"

"I know there may not be a direct connection, but it is highly unlikely that someone other than Lael accidentally used the inner pouch of a bag for which she had the matching satchel and filled it with money before then storing it in a house that she was renting to her father and her stepmother." Finley laid out her logic and then waited for the others to poke holes in it. "I don't know if that much coincidence is even possible."

The others' silence suggested they agreed. Finley had now moved past whether Lael was involved to what exactly she was involved in. Was she the owner of the money? *Looks so, if the satchel connection holds.* Was the money legal? *Probably not, since she had it hidden.* Is the money the reason for the bones? *Hard to say. Depends on when she started putting the money there, why, and whether her father—and her stepmother—knew.*

"This is getting too complicated. And sad, if family is indeed involved." Finley's mind reconnected with the group. "For the time being, we should just leave it. I say let's decide on dessert, head back to the house, and confirm our plans for the bachelor and bachelorette parties for tomorrow! Whitt and David, you two can make yourselves scarce by the pool while we're talking!"

As was the new routine, Max and Finley were enjoying their coffee beside the pool the next morning when the others pulled themselves out of bed. The party planning had concluded quickly and been overtaken by bourbon and champagne poolside, which lasted into the wee hours of the morning. Finley was glad that the houses on both sides of them were empty. The laughter and friendly conversation were more than lively at times. In any other city, the decibel level might have resulted in a conversation with the cops, but in the Holy City in May, when a lot of the college students were graduating and a lot of young couples were getting married, this sort of partying was to be expected.

"How do you do it?" Logan slowly dragged himself onto the patio, while Hema followed behind carrying two mugs of coffee. "Hema's not much better. Always chipper in the morning, planning out the day. She needs to think about her plans more quietly!"

"Did you take an aspirin?" Hema raised an eyebrow at Logan as she took a sip of the strong, hot coffee. "Drink your coffee. It will help your head."

Max gave Logan a half smile in sympathy. "I thought they said good champagne never gave a bad head. Glad I stuck to bourbon!"

"When you consume as much as we did, I think all bets are off as to whether good champagne can ward off a hangover," Logan murmured from behind half-closed lids. "I wonder how Whitt is doing. She gave me a good run for my money. That girl can drink!"

"Yep. It may make her drowsy but rarely sick," Finley added, as Whitt and Charlie bounded onto the patio. "My point has been proven. How're you feeling?"

"I'm fine. So's Charlie. David will be once he gets food," Whitt reported. "What about Reid? I hope he didn't make Kirsten hold his head!"

"I didn't! The aspirin and club soda took care of whatever was ailing me. If I'd had a bad head, Kirsten's snoring would have driven me to suicide," Reid had joined the crew on the patio, coffee in hand. Kirsten slipped in behind him and ribbed him for his comment about her snoring.

Kirsten took a bite of her husband's biscuit before redirecting the conversation. "So, what are the plans for today? Until party time tonight!"

"I'm going to check on the house around the corner to be sure it's ready for the Blake cousins, who should be checking in this morning. Not sure what I'm up to afterward," Finley relayed. "Whitt and David said they were going to head over to Aunt Cora and Uncle John's house to spend time with his parents. For the rest of you, there is always the pool and shopping. The formal touring will start this afternoon. We'll have carriages coming to pick you up about two thirty or so." Finley took the last gulp of her coffee and looked over at Max. "What're you going to do today?"

"Whatever you're going to do. I'm your wingman for the week." Max got up, put Finley's cup on the table, and pulled her to him. "No, make that for the rest of my life."

Finley gave in to his embrace and rested her head on his chest. "Promise?"

"Promise."

The walk over to the house on Montagu took all of three minutes. They soon found themselves in front of an imposing Charleston single with two levels of high and wide porches that fronted the house and continued down half of the right side. Tall black shutters cut the stark whiteness of the house's façade and provided symmetry. Slender round columns supported the porch and roof, with doweled fencing in between. The illusion was of a delicately iced layer cake.

Finley and Max entered the iron gate and walked up the wide graveled path that led to the front door. Sculpted miniature boxwoods edged either side of the path, adding formality to the otherwise simple landscape. Finley knocked gently before inserting the key Lael had given her. She wasn't expecting anyone to be there this early in the day, but she and Max could both hear noise coming from the kitchen as soon as they opened the door.

"Hello? Is anyone there?" Finley called out as she entered the inlaid wood vestibule and proceeded down the hall toward the kitchen. The house had a much more modern feel than the Rutledge house, both in the furniture and in the artwork. "This is Finley—just checking in."

From around the doorway that separated the dining area from the kitchen, a head popped out.

"Finley, goodness, you gave me a real scare! I guess, though, I should be apologizing to you, since we're the ones that got here early." Finley's cousin Jimmy came into full view.

He was a tall, rangy-looking man in his late thirties. As he'd grown older, he'd started to remind Finley and Whitt of a Nordic mountain man, with his chin-length dark hair and closely cropped beard, which was now flecked with a few strands of gray. He was an environmental lawyer, so the outdoorsy look suited the role.

He gave his cousin a hug before extending his hand to Max. "Jim Blake. And somewhere around here is my significant other, Laine."

Max introduced himself and stepped back to stand beside Finley. He was curious as to how she would define his relationship to her, since she hadn't liked being called his wife.

"Max is my better half," Finley explained, taking Max's hand in hers as she spoke. "When did you guys get in?"

"About an hour ago. We drove down, and it took less time than we thought. Decided to drive down at night and beat the traffic, which worked. You said a key would be under the mat, so we used it."

"We only got here early because I did most of the driving!" Laine stepped in from the sunroom. She was tall and reedy with fine, willow-brown hair she wore in a French braid that extended halfway down her back. *Her earth mother vibe is matching his mountain man pretty well. I always thought they made a cute couple.*

"Lainey! How good to see you! It's been a long while." Finley wrapped her arms around the woman and planted a kiss on her cheek.

"We'd see more of you—and your sister—if you ever stayed in the States. But no, you have to spend your days traipsing halfway around the world!" Laine teased. She turned to Max and introduced herself.

"Did you guys claim a room already? We were coming over to check that everything was ready for you." *And that there were no surprises—like bodies—lying about!* Finley thought, but she kept that idea to herself. She would have to find a way later to alert them to the fact that there might be cops stopping by periodically. "When are the others getting in?"

"Cate and crew should be in later this morning, if they didn't have too many stops with Brett. They said they were starting out early, but with a four-year-old, it's hard to say how long it's going to take."

"What about Caroline? Is she going to make it?" Finley wasn't sure her cousin Caroline would be up for the trappings of a wedding after going through a nasty divorce only months before. "And Nessa?"

Jimmy grimaced at the mention of his sister's name. She probably would have winced at the use of her childhood nickname. She went by Vanessa now that she was a high-powered investment banker in Manhattan. Unmarried, except to money, she wore her singleness more like a badge of honor than a state of normal existence. Most conversations with Nessa were sprinkled with her castigation of men, personally, professionally, and in society. *There must be something deep that's fueling that sort of anger*, Finley mused. Finley rarely saw her, except at family gatherings like this, and that was fine. While Whitt tolerated Nessa better than most, Finley— and apparently her own brother—were not particularly fond of her; they had never been able to find common ground.

"Caroline will get in about noon today. And Nessa is flying in tomorrow around the same time," Jimmy reported.

"Well, if you get bored, you can walk around the corner and join us by the pool. We have a crazy mix of characters. Then again, if you're looking for peace and quiet, you might want to claim the calm here. You won't find it over there!"

"We'll probably wait for Cate and Caroline before we head around." Jimmy looked at Laine for confirmation. She nodded.

"That's fine. Let me know if there is anything you need. Lael seems to have done a good job getting the houses ready, though." Finley and Max said their goodbyes and headed toward the door.

Finley was almost out the door and onto the porch before she hesitated. *Now is as good a time as any.* "Oh, by the way, you might see police cars around the Rutledge place—and the Sullivan house, too, as a matter of fact." Finley's face registered an apology. "We had a couple of incidents, here and in Beaufort, that the police are looking into."

"What sort of incidents?" Laine stepped forward in curiosity.

"Some bones in Beaufort, and a body in the closet over at Rutledge," Finley explained. "But the police say they have it under control."

15

'M SORRY." IT WAS JIMMY now who let curiosity take over. He didn't seem alarmed, just quizzical. "Bones *and* a body?"

Finley nodded. Max stepped back inside the door. They weren't going to get away without an explanation, he knew. Max wondered how much Finley was going to tell them. Given that she headed into the dining room, pulled out a chair, and sat down, it appeared she planned to tell them pretty much all of it.

Finley was just finishing the Rutledge house tale when a minivan pulled up to the front of the house. There was a pause before a slender woman of average height with dark, blunt-cut, chin-length hair got out and slid open the rear door of the car. Her wispy bangs covered much of the large, round sunglasses she wore. The last time Finley and Whitt had seen their cousin Cate Betterman Lyons was shortly after the birth of Brett. Finley had been back in New York after returning from Tangier the first time and had just made partner. A weekend trip home to Chevy Chase had resulted in a drive out to Cate and Archer's house in Leesburg to see the new baby.

Cate leaned into the back seat and unbuckled a little girl in blue shorts and a rainbow T-shirt. The child quickly grabbed a stuffed toy rabbit and hopped out of the vehicle. The "new baby" was a big girl now.

"They made pretty good time!" Jimmy and Laine stood and headed toward the door to greet the new arrivals. "You're going to have to put a pause in the story," Jimmy said. "I know Cate will want to hear this."

Max and Finley followed the other two out to the sidewalk. Max, the only one without a history with the group, was introduced. Soon Cate, Jimmy, and Laine returned to the dining table to listen to Finley and Max recount the story of the bones and the body. Archer, Cate's husband, decided that he would catch Cate's replay of the events later and headed to the backyard to play with Brett.

"So, you still have no idea whose bones those are?" Laine rested her head sideways on her palm, letting her arm carry the weight, as if the information just shared had made her skull too heavy to be supported by her neck alone. "Do you know who the body belonged to?"

Finley was slow to respond, casting a glance at Max before she answered. "Yes, the police have identified the body. It was Tommy, a cousin on my mother's side."

At that, Cate and Laine both gasped. "Finley, I'm so sorry," Jimmy murmured. "Do they have any idea how it happened? Was it a heart attack? An accident?"

"No, unfortunately, he appears to have been murdered. Blunt force trauma to the head," Finley said quietly, staring at the wood grain patterns in the table.

She didn't know why recounting this information to her cousins had suddenly become so unsettling. She had never liked Tommy and had tried to avoid him as much as she could. Was it because she felt that she was supposed to be upset, or was there some other underlying reason? *It's the violence of his death—and presumably of the death of the person that the bones belong to. Yes, it's the violence of those deaths that's rattling me. There was anger in the wound that killed Tommy. Real anger.*

Finley continued, "And the way the bones were found also suggests murder. Hence the police presence. I just wanted you all to know so that you weren't puzzled if you saw police around."

"Poor Whitt. Some wedding celebration," Cate whispered. "How's she holding up?"

"Surprisingly well. Some anxiety, but we have been trying to distract her with outings and activities," Finley shared. "In fact, there will be carriage tours of the historic parts of Charleston this afternoon. And the bachelor and bachelorette parties this evening. We'll have the carriages pull around here to pick you all up a little after two thirty. The parties will start around seven."

Finley pushed back from the table, and Max followed her lead. "We'd better get out of your hair and let you guys settle in. We'll see you on the tour. Can't wait to see Caroline when she gets in."

Finley and Max showed themselves to the door. The Blake cousins barely acknowledged their departure, they were so deep into a state of confusion over the revelations of bodies and bones.

"You slipped the murders in pretty smoothly, if I may say so, sweetheart." Max took her hand in his as they walked down the block toward the Rutledge house. "That couldn't have been easy. I know you weren't fond of the guy, but he was family."

"Yeah. I figured it was better to put it out in the open. Trying to hide it wasn't going to work, as much as I'm sure Mama will be mortified that I talked death with them so shortly after their arrival. I'll bet she hasn't even mentioned anything about it to David's people."

"David and Whitt are probably dealing with it now."

"You don't think guests will start leaving because of this, do you?"

"Most of the guests will arrive the morning of the wedding, and by then, you—and the police, of course—will have it solved."

Finley turned to Max. "Be serious! This is Whitt's wedding!"

"I am being serious—that most people won't even know. And half-serious that you'll have it solved." Max wrapped his arm around her waist and pulled her to him. He kissed her head before slipping her arm through his for the remainder of the walk home. "It'll be fine, trust me."

It'd been a while since Finley had taken one of the Charleston guided carriage rides. She and Whitt must have still been in grade school when they'd accompanied their parents in a horse-drawn surrey with fringe through the narrow streets of the old city. At that time, the city had been less congested with tourist traffic, so the itinerary around the historic part of the city had been shared in advance. This time, because of traffic regulations, the route of the carriage was determined by the police only moments before the drivers took off.

The Montagu house crew had walked the short distance over to the other house on Rutledge, ostensibly to save the carriage drivers an extra stop. But Cate finally shared the real reason as she gushed over the splendor of the houses on both Montagu and Rutledge.

"Okay, we were curious if it was possible to get a house more splendid than the one we're in, but I think this one matches it," she said, as she entered the foyer of the Rutledge house. Where the Montagu house had a center vestibule from which all the other rooms flowed, the Rutledge house was guided by the main hallway that ran like a spine down the center of the house, opening to the sunroom, dining room, and main parlor before spilling into the kitchen, a small study, and a den.

Having all the cousins and friends in one place when the carriages came allowed Finley and Whitt to divide the group so that the wedding party could get to know each other as they were touring. Whitt was sorry that David's sister, Tierney, wasn't able to join them for the prewedding festivities, but medical school exams had her occupied until right before the wedding. She might even have to miss the rehearsal dinner. She promised she would be at the wedding, though. "Even if I have to steal a witch's broom to get there," she had joked.

The carriages arrived right on time. Caroline dropped her bags at the Montagu house and hurried around the corner to catch the group as they were loading up. Finley met her with a hug as she joined the small crowd outside the Rutledge house.

"Slow down! We weren't going to leave you," Finley called to the woman, who looked identical to Cate, her twin sister, but for the longer length of her hair and the lack of sunglasses. "We would have waited for you. How was your flight?"

Caroline unwound her niece, Brett, who had rushed to greet her, from around her legs and picked up the little girl. "Hello to you too, little one! You excited about the horses, Bretty? Do you know their names yet?" Holding the child as she petted the horse, Caroline turned her attention back to Finley. "The flight down was fine. Short, which was all that mattered. So, which one is the groom?"

Finley pointed to David before calling Whitt and David over for introductions. When the two carriages finally departed for the ninety-minute trip around the old town, Finley and Max had joined Charlie, Mooney, and Ian in the fringe-rimmed chariot that also carried Caroline and Brett. The child had latched herself onto her aunt since she'd arrived and followed her like a shadow. Caroline had let Brett decide which horse she wanted to ride with and then climbed in to join her.

"I like horses," Brett announced, as the carriage started off. She peered over the back of the bench on which Max and Finley were sitting, her chin in her hands. Her eyes never left Max's face. She seemed curious about him, watching him like a cat, with only her eyes moving, as he settled into his seat. "My grandma has horses."

Max paused in his movements when he realized she'd addressed her comment to him directly. He turned his head slightly to look at her. "Does she, now? What are their names?"

"I can't remember," she shared in her tiny voice. "Do you have a grandma?"

Max smiled at the little girl as he responded, modulating his words so they didn't sound harsh in their revelation. "I did, but she died."

"Oh. She did?" Brett paused and tilted her little head toward Max. "Who killed her?"

Max's face froze. Caroline, who had been talking to Charlie, stopped midphrase. Ian stared bug-eyed at Mooney, who was choking in order to stifle a laugh. Ben, the young guide for the tour, almost dropped the reins.

Finley recovered first. "No one, sweetheart. She was old."

They all watched as the child considered that and nodded a confirmation. "She was old." Brett then nonchalantly climbed into her aunt's lap and was soon asleep.

Mooney could contain herself no longer and broke into loud guffaws that soon became contagious. The carriage traveled several blocks before the group regained composure.

"Where did that come from?" Ian asked, shifting his glance from Mooney, who was still snickering, to Brett, who was curled up innocently in Caroline's arms.

"I haven't the slightest idea!" Caroline whispered, shaking her head. "Too much television?"

"Goodness only knows. But that is a story we'll be telling for a very long time!" Max declared. "'Who killed her?'"

"Out of the mouth of babes!" Charlie chortled. "Who knew!"

The rest of the trip was uneventful. Eloise, the Belgian carriage horse that Brett was so enamored with, clomped along the cobbled street as if programmed. Ben shared the rich and sometimes sordid history of the area, and Max punctuated Ben's informative, often funny narrative with questions that prompted additional facts given. Through it all, Brett slept, rousing herself periodically to look around before burrowing into Caroline's arms again and falling back asleep.

At one point, Finley could have sworn she saw her cousin Lael. She was leaning on a black pickup truck, talking to a guy in a gray

T-shirt and jeans, near some apartments on Wentworth. It seemed to Finley that the guy didn't want to be seen, since every time someone went by on foot or in a car, he pulled his baseball cap further down over his forehead.

Finley quickly decided that the woman couldn't have been Lael, despite the match in height and hair color, because the woman in question was in jeans, something Finley had never seen her cousin wear. Perhaps more confirming of Finley's misidentification was the fact that the woman's hair was pulled back into a severe ponytail, something Lael would never do to her perfectly coiffed mane.

Finley wished Whitt had been there so she could have called Finley crazy once again for her imaginary sightings, but Whitt was in the other carriage several blocks behind. To text her would have been a bit extreme. She quickly snapped a picture and then returned to the conversation. *I'll ask Whitt later.*

"That was probably the best class on American history I've had in my life," Max remarked as the tour concluded. "I always preferred European history to American, but that may change now. Thanks!"

Ben's carriage deposited its occupants in front of the Rutledge house and then waited for the other coach to arrive. Finley and Caroline had arranged for Ben to wait for Jimmy, Laine, Cate, and Archer so that he could transport them all over to the Montagu house, since Brett was still napping. However, as soon as the carriage stopped, Brett was wide awake.

As the carriage with the Blake cousins pulled away, Finley and Whitt stood on the front stairs of the house, waving a short farewell. Brett returned their send-off with her version of the Queen's wave.

"So, Mama and Daddy are coming across the bridge just to look after Brett?" Whitt sounded puzzled as she continued to stare after the coach until it rounded the corner, out of sight.

"Yep," Finley responded cryptically.

"Why?" Whitt continued to probe. "Just to give her parents a break? We can look after her if we all go out to dinner together. She isn't a difficult child. We can take turns keeping an eye on her."

Finley considered Brett's precociousness earlier in the day and smiled to herself. "There are just some places you don't take children, Whitt." Finley paused. "And we'll be going to some of those places tonight."

With the last comment, the lightbulb in Whitt's brain switched on. "Oh! Oh! Now I get it. This is bachelorette night! Goodness, I almost forgot!"

"Forgot! How could you forget your almost last night of single-hood!" Finley cried, wrapping her arms around her sister's shoulders. "Two more nights, little sis, and you will be an old married lady!"

Whitt's face erupted into a huge grin before the tears began. "Yep, I'm getting married. I'm so happy I could I burst!"

Finley tightened her embrace on her sister. The two of them stood on the front steps holding each other, washed in happy tears, until Max stuck his head out the door. "You two okay?"

"Fine," Finley mouthed, but she maintained her hold on her sister. After a moment, Max nodded and took his leave. *I bet we look like fools out here, but who the heck cares. My baby sister is getting married. To the second-best guy on the planet! I've got the first.*

Two party vans pulled up to the Rutledge house just after seven. The "stags" were headed to Edmund's Oast, a craft brewery, for a beer tasting and tour before dinner. Max had then planned for them—the groomsmen plus an odd mix of cousins, classmates, and frat brothers who had arrived to send David out in style—to head to a backroom at Victor Social Club for the rest of the night. The details had been spotty, and Finley hadn't asked for more.

For the "hens," Finley had planned a mix of activities, things that Whitt had either always liked or had said were on her bucket list. The bridesmaids and girlfriends had been in the van for less than five minutes before the driver dropped them off behind a bright-pink bakery storefront.

"Ladies, welcome! Come on in! Don't be shy. We're going to have a good time tonight!" a man announced as the women disembarked. He was of ageless features and genteel mannerisms, dressed in the Southern gentleman's summer uniform of khaki pants and striped button-down, to which he'd added a jaunty paisley bowtie. "Sally and I are going to make sure that you have the best of times!"

He turned to a petite woman in her midforties. Although she was casually dressed in black slacks and an ice-blue, cross-tied polished-cotton blouse, she was perfectly turned out, from her manicured nails to her Turkish embroidered mules.

"This is my sister, Sally, and I'm Teddy! We're your coordinators for this evening, so if there is anything that you need, want, or even wish you had, we're here to provide it. We're your fairy godmothers!" Teddy waved his imaginary wand dramatically and tittered.

Sally took the floor. She was Teddy's counterpart. For all his camp theatrics, she was a sugarcoated GI Jane—straightforward, under control, in charge, delivered with the sweetest Miss Scarlett accent, of course. "As Teddy said, we want you to have fun tonight." She directed her gaze at Whitt. "If you are lucky, dear, you will only get married once. So, let's make this special."

As she spoke, she draped a bright-pink "Future Mrs." sash over Whitt's head. Whitt winced a little, both at the color and the saying. Meanwhile, Teddy passed among the other women, handing out matching sashes with the words "I Do Crew" on them. Several other cousins, largely from the Montgomery side, had joined the bridal party for the fun, Lael among them.

"We're going to start the fun with a scavenger hunt! This one is one of the most unusual ones I've ever conducted. I had to look up some of the things on it!" Teddy arched an eyebrow at Finley, who had made some of those quirky additions to match Whitt's life experience.

The mention of a scavenger hunt brought a silly grin to Whitt's face. It brought back memories of summers with Finley and her parents in far-off places and scrambled requests for the listed treasures in pidgin versions of whatever language was spoken in that country. *Daddy's crazy attempt to force us to use our schoolgirl French or German. I guess it worked. We can at least order in a restaurant throughout much of the world.*

Sally organized the horde into deployable platoons. She wandered the room with a small bucket filled with scraps of paper. "Grab a number, and we'll form teams."

Damn. I said any team but Lael's and what do I get? Lael. Better me than Whitt, Finley thought. The luck of the draw had Lael, Finley, and Charlie making up one of the five teams. Teddy handed out the list of items to be scavenged, gave the instructions, and sounded the gong. With that, the groups of women bolted from the pretty little party room and raced down the street.

"Let's approach this strategically," Lael began in her languid drawl. "Let's dump out our bags and see what we have already."

The others nodded at the strategy and started emptying the contents of their bags. The team was able to knock off several items immediately. Finley unzipped the side pocket of her satchel and pulled out currency from three different countries—the UK, India, and Morocco—to which Charlie added Philippine pesos, Laotian kip, Singaporean dollars, and Thai baht.

Charlie also pulled a guitar pick from her wallet and laid it on the table. "What self-respecting guitarist would leave home without a handful of picks?" Finley recalled that Whitt had talked about Charlie's musical prowess as the lead guitarist and vocalist of a blues and rock band she had helped form in Manila, the Raiders.

Lael rummaged through the displayed items from her bag— lipstick, an eye pencil, a small notebook and pen, her wallet, a fan, a foldable shopping bag, a pencil case, and a clear plastic portfolio overflowing with papers and receipts. From this cache, Lael was able to contribute to the scavenger list a nail file, a receipt for a "durable item of more than $500 in value"—which turned out to be a refrigerator for one of the units she managed—and a pack of false eyelashes. As Lael sorted through the items, Finley's eye fell on a coin purse in a lovely Victorian floral and two sets of keyrings, full of loyalty cards and house and car keys. One set was held together by an ornate keyring designed with stylized initials. She looked up to Lael's penetrating gaze.

"Brilliant strategy, Lael. Great start. We'd better catch up to the others." Finley dropped her eyes and hurriedly shoved the contents of her bag back into the pockets and folds. She gave a wan smile. "You know, we might just win this thing!"

16

THE NEXT MORNING, FINLEY AND Max had been up for at least an hour when the Beaufort police called to update them on the bones in the attic. The police remembered that they were to relay all requests to Finley, per Daddy's instruction. *No way are they going to throw Mama and Whitt into a tizzy this close to the wedding. I would come after them with a hatchet if they did!* The officer said that they had been able to trace the previous tenant, Elijah Hale. He was indeed Albertine's ex-husband and Lael's father. He was also dead!

Finley had moved to the sunroom when the police called to avoid Whitt hearing the conversation. Max understood that his job was to distract Whitt should she wander down the stairs looking for her sister. Finley gasped audibly at the news that Buster was dead. *Another thing to add to the list of things to tell Mama and Whitt after the wedding—long after the wedding!*

"How did he die? And when?" Finley thought of the bones that had fallen from the attic and wondered if Buster had also withered to dust.

"It appears to have been natural causes. Most likely a heart attack, but we don't have the coroner's report yet. He'd only been dead a few weeks when we tracked him down. He was back in Edisto. Some friends said they let him bunk in their spare bedroom and found him dead one morning," the officer named Ned stated. "They reported it, but the names were different. It wasn't until you called to say Elijah and Buster were the same person that we made the connection."

"So, what happens now?" Finley was trying to figure out how, with the initial suspected victim dead, they were ever going to find out whose bones they were. "Do you have any idea where the bones came from and who the deceased was?"

"No, ma'am, that part of the investigation is still underway." With that, the officer rang off.

"Well, that was singularly unhelpful," Finley muttered to herself, as she wandered back into the kitchen.

"What was?" Max asked, having heard the end of her conversation with herself.

"That Buster is dead and the bones are still unidentified!" Finley explained.

"Dead?" Max stopped midpour of his second cup of coffee. "How many bodies have you racked up this time? Four? Five?"

Finley took the carafe from his hand, finished pouring his cup, and then topped off hers. "Don't exaggerate. It's only three, and one was natural causes—at least, they think Buster's was a heart attack."

Max chuckled to himself. Only with the Blake sisters could a body count greater than zero be viewed as within the range of normal.

"At least there is nothing to get in the way of the rehearsal dinner tonight or the wedding tomorrow. These guys, unlike the cops here, don't think any of us have anything to do with it. So, we should be free and clear!"

Max picked up Finley's cup and started for the pool deck. "If you say so," he mumbled under his breath, clearly unconvinced.

When they reached the pool, Max pulled Finley's lounge chair closer to his and set the coffee on the side table between them. "Did you have fun last night? You were asleep when I got in."

"I should be asking you," Finley arched an eyebrow at Max. "You alley cats crawled home well after three. Did you shut the place down?"

"Almost, but not quite. The bar closed at three, and we headed home around two thirty. Wasted! Definitely wasted." Max shook his head with a wry grin at the memory of the night before. "Some more wasted than others."

"This is why Mama insisted that all the partying be done in advance of the wedding. You'd better be closemouthed about all this. Mama would have a hissy fit if she found out," Finley cautioned.

"I would imagine, but we were all of age and there was no property damage," Max retorted. "Besides, it was all good, clean fun. Drunken, but clean! What about you? What did you ladies do? Strip club? Shirtless guys in police uniforms?"

"Gross! Whitt would have walked out if we had tried any of that." Finley turned to Max, wide-eyed, visions of scantily clad women doing lap dances flashing before her. "You guys didn't, did you?"

Max smiled slyly before responding, "Whatever happens in Charleston, stays in Charleston." He paused. "But no. As I said before, it was just clean fun. His frat brothers ratting him out, making him do shots, that sort of thing. But you still haven't told me what you did? Was it that naughty?"

Finley imagined poor David taking the teasing in his laid-back, easy style and his speech becoming more languid and California dreamy with each shot. She knew Max had paced himself in his always-in-control manner, which was why he was lucid this morning.

"We did a bridal scavenger hunt. It's been one of Whitt's favorite things to do ever since she was little. We were all decked out in pink sashes and tiaras, running around the city asking strangers for $2 bills and unlit white wedding tapers," Finley laughed. "My team won, as it turns out!"

Her smile faded as she continued. "Lael was on my team. With Charlie, thank God. But the odd thing is that a coin purse that Lael had in her satchel made me think of the pattern on one of the bags that fell from the ceiling at the Beaufort house," Finley recounted. "I mentioned it to the police this morning. It was the same floral pattern that was on the tote bag Lael was carrying the other day."

"Are you sure?" Max took a slow sip of his coffee, eyeing Finley over the top of his cup. "A lot of patterns are similar but have slight variations. I'd hate for you to accuse your cousin of murder based on that."

"I'm not accusing her of murder. Goodness, no. I'm just saying that the fact she said the satchel had other pieces including a pouch that was missing, that a similar floral pouch with a lot of money in it was found, and that all that money was in a house she was renting to her daddy are things that need to be investigated," Finley clarified.

"And take a look at this." Finley paused the conversation while she ran inside and grabbed her camera. She scrolled through the frames until she got to the picture she'd taken of the Lael look-alike. "Now tell me that isn't Lael!"

Max glanced at the photo and then touched the screen to zoom in on the shot. "I don't know about the woman, but that looks like the same guy who was following us the other day. The hat's the same, unusual color of blue."

Finley took a second look and, after a long pause, nodded. "I told you, something ain't right—and Lael's involved!"

Max remained silent for a moment before adding, "Maybe, but tell me the fact that you aren't her biggest fan isn't playing into this?"

Finley smirked slightly. "Well, maybe just a little. Getting her in a bit of hot water would be fair play given the hell she gave Whitt and me. That said, the facts don't lie." Finley turned serious again. "The other thing that bothered me was the way she looked at me when she caught me staring at the coin purse. I'll say it again: something's not right."

"Well, you told the police. And now you can show them the picture and tell them we were being followed. Then you need to refocus on the wedding!" Max reminded her. "What's the plan for today?"

"You guys get to sleep off your bad heads while we ladies in the wedding party head over to Aunt Cora and Uncle John's. She and Mama are throwing Whitt a bridal luncheon at her house at noon. Then we are scheduled to take a tour of Fort Sumter this afternoon, before the rehearsal party," Finley outlined. "So as long as you and David are at Mama and Daddy's house by six for the rehearsal, you have the whole day to yourselves."

"I have my orders, ma'am, and I will make sure that he is at rehearsal." Max play saluted Finley before leaning over to kiss her gently.

"You two need to quit! Every time you're together—which is all the time—you're pawing and preening each other!" Whitt stood at the patio door.

"You've got a lot of nerve talking about PDA!" Finley teased. "There is coffee made, and some cinnamon buns are in the oven. They should almost be ready to be taken out. Check them for me, please?"

"Gladly!" Whitt exclaimed, as she headed back into the kitchen for coffee and cinnamon buns.

Whitt complained that between the bride's lunch, the tour of Fort Sumter, the rehearsal, and the dinner following it, the day was going to have more dress changes than an opera at the Met. After breakfast and some sunning by the pool, the hens in the clutch joined Mama and sundry girl cousins at the Davis house for the bride's lunch. Mama and Aunt Cora had paid attention to even the smallest detail.

Guests were met at the door with Kir Miradors, a cocktail of champagne blushed by a raspberry and a touch of Solerno blood orange liqueur that tinted the bubbly the exact blush of Whitt's wedding color palette.

Kirsten grumbled about having to take sparkling cider instead of the bubbly cocktail. "When these suckers are out, delivered, and healthy, I'm going to drink a whole case of the real stuff!" she vowed, pointing at her expanded belly.

The hostesses had stayed true to Whitt's blush, celadon, and gray color scheme and mounded the tables with small pots of Angel Cheeks peonies and gray-green succulents. Aunt Cora and Mama had decided on individual cake pulls rather than a big cake with multiple pulls. Each place was set with a small, glazed Bundt cake from which ran a pale-pink ribbon. According to tradition, the charm that each guest pulled from the cake foretold their future—a cradle meant babies, a ring signaled a walk down the aisle, a horse-shoe promised good luck. In the New Orleans tradition, there were eight charms, each foreshadowing the future. However, Mama always removed the penny (poverty) and the thimble (spinsterhood) from the charm pack, switching them out for other charms. "No poor girl needs to have all hope for a decent future crushed. That's too cruel. A young lady should always be able to dream."

After a sumptuous lunch of curried chicken salad, ham bis-cuits, fennel apple salad, assorted cheeses, and the obligatory cheese straws and benne wafers, the assembled ladies were ready for the pull. Finley watched as each woman in the party pulled their ribbon to reveal their fate. As the matron of honor, she pulled last. She colored red when the end of her pull revealed a cradle. *Whitt set me up. I know she did!*

"I'll save the baby clothes and bouncy seat for you!" Kirsten called from across the table.

After the pull, the guests took their cake and coffee and moved to the terrace that overlooked the water. Finley took one of the remaining seats closest to the water's edge, mindful that it came with a cost. It was beside Lael, who sat sipping another glass of champagne, looking pensively out to sea.

"What charm did you get?" Finley ventured, trying to make polite conversation and hoping that Lael didn't remember the awkward exchange the night before.

Finley had been unable to tell why Lael had been eying her. *She wouldn't have seen the pouch at the Beaufort house or known that we made a connection between her bag and the money pouch. So there was something else that had her spooked. Whatever it was, be polite. This wedding will soon be over, and she'll be gone!*

"She got the telephone! Harbinger of good news!" Mama interjected. "Which reminded me that your sister said the Beaufort police called. Sorry to interrupt, Lael sweetheart, but I want to be sure Finley understands that if the police want to talk to us, it will have to be after the wedding!"

"Why ever would the police want to talk to you, Auntie?" Lael turned and looked up at Mama, who had positioned herself between the two young women.

"Oh, dear, you wouldn't have heard about it." Mama clasped her hand to her chest and shook her head. "Not the thing you want to talk about at a bride's lunch, but the long and short of it is that when we went to look over the little house in Beaufort, we found some bones and a lot of money in the attic. Needless to say, the police are investigating."

Finley was glad that Mama was called away before she could say more. The shift in Lael's countenance signaled that Mama had said something important. Finley had no idea which part of the conversation had alarmed Lael, but something had.

"Are you going with us to Fort Sumter this afternoon? One last tour before the rehearsal." Finley tried to change the subject to recover the conversation. "We are booked on the two-thirty boat. You should come on down. Should be fun!"

Finley watched as Lael tried to register enough of what Finley had said to offer a reasoned response, even as the better part of her mind space was occupied by something else.

"Maybe. I'll have to see," Lael answered distractedly. "Look I hate to eat and run, but I have a million things I need to do, and your mama made me remember a big something that had slipped my mind. See you at the rehearsal dinner!"

Finley had barely nodded in response before Lael was gone. *She is such a strange person. Something Mama said rattled her, that's for sure. Kind of glad that she's gone, though. I can stop being so fricking polite. That was hard work!*

Whitt and Finley were glad they had told those in the Charleston houses to grab the clothes they would need for the rest of the day—for the boat ride over to Sumter and then for the rehearsal dinner—since time between events was likely to be tight. At just before two, there was a mad scramble for the bathrooms as ten-plus women tried to change clothes. David's mother drew Whitt and Finley into the bedroom she was staying in and allowed them to make a quick change there.

The short ride down to the dock sounded like the back of the summer camp van, with high-pitched laughter, some women talking over each other, and others singing to the music way too loud.

"Do you think they are going to let us on the boat? We look like a bunch of drunken sailors!" Whitt assessed after surveying the group in the chartered van.

"If they let the guys on, they had better let us on. According to Max, those are the ones who are pickled," Finley replied.

When the van pulled up to the ferry dock, Max and David were passing out seasickness pills to the assembled group of men—David's groomsmen, his frat brothers, and the assorted Montgomery and Blake cousins.

Max looked up when the women disembarked. He planted a kiss on Finley's cheek when she came over. "You ladies have a nice lunch?"

Before Finley could answer, the ferryman cried out, "Let's load up!"

The thirty-minute ferry ride out to the island fortification was an excursion in itself. Gliding out into the mouth of the harbor from Mount Pleasant, the ferry passed the USS Yorktown, now anchored in an inlet off the Cooper River. As the vessel moved farther out into the water, dolphins arced from the water like a synchronized swimming team. When the boat neared the fort, the dolphin welcoming committee broke off and continued out to sea.

"We could have cut the travel time in half and just left from Sullivan's," Whitt remarked, looking at a map of the location in her guidebook, which placed Fort Sumter National Park just off the coast of Sullivan's Island.

"Yeah, and then spent the night before your wedding in a jail cell," David joked. "It's illegal for anyone but National Park Service concessionaires to travel out to the island."

"Smarty-pants!" Whitt responded with a smirk, before going back to reading about the park, which captured the history of the buildup to and opening salvo of the Civil War, the bloodiest war of United States.

"There aren't any formal tours out here. Grab a map and brochure when you get off the boat and wander around. The Park rangers are quite knowledgeable and can answer any of your questions. And be sure to check out the museum shop!" the captain announced over the loudspeaker.

As the ferry slipped quietly into the dock, he continued. "We leave the dock and head back to Mount Pleasant at 4:00 p.m. on the dot, and this is the last boat back. So, unless you want to spend the night out here—with the ghosts—I suggest you return to the dock in advance of our departure!"

Max placed his hand at the small of Finley's back and guided her down the gangplank to the path that led to the battlements. Huge black cannons dotted the landscape, leaving no doubt what the island had been. Crumbling stone arches, bearing testament to the bombardment that signaled the start of the Civil War, encircled a large center green that was crisscrossed with stone paths.

"Which way do you want to go?" Max asked, as they stopped at a panoramic map of the site. Whitt, David, and Charlie soon joined them.

"Doesn't really matter. If we wander in a circle, we are bound to cover everything. We can't really get lost—we're on an island!" Finley responded. The others chuckled.

With that, the group struck off, stopping to read the extensive descriptions of the historical setting and the building action that resulted in the surrender of Fort Sumter. After a time, Whitt and Finley found themselves together in their meandering walk around the ruins of the fort.

"Let's see what's over here," Whitt motioned toward an arch that led to a path to the sea. "Do you have your camera? You might be able to get some nice shots from this side."

Finley followed her sister through the arch and around to a narrow outcropping of rocks that jutted from the fortress's rear. What the building lacked in architectural appeal it made up for in its positioning on the rocks. Finley relished her return to the view from behind the camera. It felt like it'd been months since she had really seen the world—from her viewfinder. In reality, it had only been several days. *But this feels good. Natural. One more day, then Max and I can head down the coast, and I can shoot some frames of the countryside.*

Finley pulled her eye away from the camera and started to talk to her sister, but the expression on Whitt's face prompted her to stop midsentence. "Whitt, you okay? What is…?"

Finley fully expected her sister to point to a water moccasin or giant spider, both of which would have posed a problem but not an insurmountable one. Instead, Finley followed Whitt's gaze and found Lael—holding a gun.

17

"**G**ood Lord, I thought I'd never get you two separated from the rest of that bunch. Clingy, aren't you?" Lael snickered. "I thought it was just your Mama's side, but it seems all of you hang onto each other like leeches. One of the benefits of being the odd woman out—don't have to tolerate family you really don't like just because they're family. And I sure as hell don't need them!"

Lael motioned with the gun for the sisters to head back through the arch through which they'd come. She then directed them down a stairway that had lost its rail as well as several bricks on many of the risers. At the bottom of the stairs, she paused, checking her direction. After a few moments, she pointed them to a narrow corridor that led to a row of gated cells. There she resumed talking.

"What used to be the brig! Good a place as any to leave you." Lael smirked at the sisters, who stood side by side. "Always so perfect. The tanned Bobbsey Twins—that's what Tommy and I used to call you!"

Before she could stop herself, Finley blurted, "But I thought you said you didn't know him that well?"

Lael laughed. "Good catch! But no extra points! I knew Tommy too well. So sorry I had to trim the only one that was my kind, but then he also started getting too clingy, wanting more. Must be a genetic flaw in the Montgomery line!" Her lip curled into a sneer. "He just outlasted his usefulness. If I had the time, I should probably kill you, too, you are so bothersome. But I need to get out of here, or I won't have time to change clothes. Lucky, aren't you? But then, you always were!"

Finley ushered her sister into the cell before her. Whitt's face hid her fear; what was evident instead was an underlying contempt for Lael that she was struggling to mask. *Wipe that look off your face, sister mine, or you are going to get us killed. I know you think she's unhinged—and she clearly is—but now ain't the time to tell her!*

"Humor me before you go!" Finley decided to distract Lael until Whitt could gain greater control over her facial expressions. Also, she really did want to know how Lael was involved in all of this. "Help me understand. Why did you kill Tommy? Neediness isn't a crime."

"Tommy found out about the bribes and kickbacks I was taking from a range of city officials and contractors for various projects and started blackmailing me. He came for his money that morning and asked me for more. I'd had it, so I hit him with an andiron. And he died." Lael's eyes were vacant, as if she was recounting a story in which she had never been involved. Just words. No emotion.

Lael snapped back to reality and focused an angry glare on Finley. "But don't play dumb. Don't play me for a fool. I knew you had it figured out when you saw the keys the other night. Stupid mistake! Stupid! And then when your mama mentioned the bones and the money in the Beaufort house, I knew it was all coming apart and I had to get out of here. In fact, I'm wasting time talking to you."

That was what had triggered the change in Lael's demeanor the night of the scavenger hunt. The keys. The two sets of keys. And the initialed key ring. TWP. Those weren't Lael's keys. *I didn't get it then, but she thought I did. That's why she thinks she has to get rid of us—or at least get us out of the way while she makes a run for it.*

Whitt had been watching Lael during the exchange with Finley. She noticed that Lael had relaxed when telling her story, like she needed to tell this to someone, to get everything she had been suppressing out in the open. Whitt took this as her cue. "Lael, did you kill your daddy and stepmother?" Her voice was low and soft, inviting even.

Lael leveled her gaze at Whitt. "Kill him? No, I didn't kill him. He probably killed himself. He was a weak man. My mama said some friends from home called to let her know he was dead. She said it was a heart attack, but he probably offed himself rather than be humiliated. As far as I'm concerned, the blackmail money was just payback for all the hell he put me and my mama through."

"Blackmail money? You were blackmailing him?" Whitt asked.

Finley was puzzled now. Mama had said Albertine had been taking money from him so his bigamy wouldn't be revealed, but what was Lael blackmailing him for? Surely not the same thing! *Bad enough to be taken by both your ex-wife and your daughter, but surely not for the same thing? That would be too sad.*

Lael's lip inched up into a twisted half smile as her eyebrow arched. "Yep. Turns out my mama and I both were. Ain't life a bitch! She got him on the bigamy, but I caught him in a bigger lie. All these years, I kept telling myself that he was coming back. That he loved me and we were his real family. I just knew he was coming back. But he never did.

"I even believed that was why he killed Lynette, that witch of a wife of his. So that he could come back to us." For a second, Lael looked like a wide-eyed child who refused to believe that a parent would disappoint her. But in a moment, her face returned to a hardened, cynical glare.

"One day, he was supposed to have gone fishing, so I let myself into the house to put some bribe money in the attic. That's where I had been stashing it," Lael recounted. "Anyway, he comes back and thinks I know about Lynette and starts telling me about how she found out about the bigamy and was threatening to go to the congregation and how he killed her. It wasn't *us* that made him kill her. He did it to save his own skin. So, I made him pay up. That simple."

Lael reached into her bag and pulled out a large padlock. "But you both ask too many questions. Just shut up and sit down. It'll take them a while to find you and by that time, I will be long gone. You always were meddlesome children, and you got even worse as adults."

Finley and Whitt did as they were told. It was safer to keep quiet. As unstable as Lael appeared, it was best to just let her go rather than risk her ire and the bullet that might come with it. The sisters watched as their cousin fastened and secured the lock. They could hear her footsteps on the pavestones as she navigated her way back up to the ground level.

"What now?" Whitt asked. "In another fifteen minutes or so, the boat is going to board and the guys will start looking for us. The rangers will likely sweep the place, after the boat has gone and the guys raise an alarm."

"But you'll be late for rehearsal and your rehearsal dinner! Which means Mama'll be spitting fire. We aren't ready to fold yet. We can still play the rest of this hand." Finley moved to the bars that secured the cell. She was impressed that Lael had done her homework and brought her own lock. She was also relieved. It was easier to pick a modern lock than a rusted nineteenth-century one.

"Got a hairpin? The one time I don't!" Finley turned to look at Whitt, who thankfully had preserved her beach waves with a few strategically placed hairpins. Whitt pulled one loose and passed it to her sister. "While I'm working on this, let's play a round of the Murder Game! We may not get to do it again for a while, once you are an old married woman!"

Whitt laughed. "If Mama can't stop us from playing, I doubt David can. So, who do you think did it?" Whitt launched into the Murder Game as easily as always. It was a game they'd created as children to occupy themselves on the trips overseas with their parents. The object of the game was to involve fellow passengers in all sorts of murderous activities and dastardly deeds.

Finley went back to the lock. "Did what? Who died and how?" Her fingers pulled open the hairpin and flattened it to form a pick. She inserted the end into the lock face and began to jiggle the pick in the lock. As she spoke, she listened to the sound of the lock.

"The woman on the boat with the purple streak in her hair."

"How?"

"Electrocution."

Finley turned to look at Whitt with surprise and bit of distaste at the choice of murder weapon. *This is a new one. Wonder what prompted that.* "Where? More importantly, what makes you say it was murder and not an accident?"

"In the kitchen. Murder, because the cord was purposely frayed. It was staged to look like an accident."

"Sloppy or bold?"

"Bold, I think, because it didn't look like any real attempt was made to cover it up."

"Did she live alone?"

"Yes. She moved out of her mama's place a few months ago. She'd been looking after her mother while she was ill."

"Any other relatives or close friends nearby?"

"Just her mother and a boyfriend, but both had alibis."

"And they ruled out the boyfriend?" Finley glanced up briefly from her work on the lock. She was pondering the facts Whitt had shared thus far.

Whitt nodded as she watched Finley continue to manipulate the lock.

"It was the mother. She had opportunity, since she probably goes in and out of the house frequently. Not too hard to short an appliance, especially one someone uses all the time. The person is unlikely to check it."

"But why? I didn't say they'd had a falling out."

"I think it was because the mother was dying and she got pissed because the daughter didn't wait until the she was gone to reassert her independence—moving out, dying her hair, etc. May be a stretch, but that's my guess."

Whitt grinned. "I thought I was being clever with the new murder weapon, but you solved it!"

"And now, we are free!"

"Well, at least in our minds we are." Whitt pulled out her phone to check the time. "We have another seven minutes before we're stuck here for the night."

"No, we really *are* free! We can make the boat. Let's go!" Finley slowly pushed open the heavy bars and headed for the stairs. As she and Whitt rounded the corner, they checked to see if they caught sight of Lael in the crowd. No sign of her.

"Where did you two get to?" David approached the sisters from the center of the green, his forehead creased with concern. He wrapped his arms around Whitt. "You had me worried."

"Thought I'd done a runner?" Whitt reached up and gently kissed her fiancé. "Wouldn't be the best place, since there's only one way off the island!"

"Whitt! You're supposed to tell him that you wouldn't ever do that. Not that you *couldn't*!" Finley teased.

"Let's get on the ferry, and then we'll explain everything." Finley touched David's shoulder as she passed.

"Are you okay?" Max joined them and slipped Finley's hand in his as his eyes scanned her face. "We looked all over for you."

"I hope you got to see some of the fort before you started looking for us." Finley squeezed Max's hand. "We got waylaid. By Lael. We need to call the police as soon as we board."

"Lael?" Max twisted both his lips and his brows. "Never mind. Make your call. If you can't get a connection, maybe the captain can radio the police for you," Max proposed, as the crew walked up the gangplank and joined the rest of the group. Max was becoming used to the sisters getting involved in some sort of mischief. The key was being sure that they could always find their way out of it once they got sucked in.

"Great idea." Finley found a seat away from the others so she could call the police. Luckily, she was able to get a signal and make the call.

When she finished talking with the police, she sent her sister a text to let her know. Whitt looked up from her conversation with Charlie and nodded. Finley hoped the police didn't detain them long; it was going to be close if they were to make it to rehearsal in time.

"You going to fill me in on what happened?" Max sat beside her, his eyes still searching for confirmation that she was all right.

Finley lowered her voice to a hoarse whisper. "Lael killed Tommy and was blackmailing her father. In addition, Lael was taking bribes. All that money was hers!"

"The money at the Beaufort house?" Max stared at Finley, slack-jawed. "Why did she kill your cousin? And were those bones her work, too?"

"No, the bones were her daddy's doing. He killed her stepmother because she was going to reveal him as a bigamist to his congregation. He'd been paying Albertine, Lael's mama, to keep quiet about the bigamy and then paying Lael to keep quiet about his second wife's murder."

Max was silent for the longest time, his eyes looking out to the horizon, his brow crinkled as he tried to process what Finley had just said. "That's crazy! And you said the money was Lael's, too?"

Finley nodded. "Yep, she'd been taking bribes and payoffs for years and storing the money in the Beaufort house since it had been empty." She moved closer to him and took his hand. "Maybe we should vow never to have children. There is too much crazy in this family!"

Max leaned over and kissed her. "I'll take my chances. Good wins out over evil in the end, and you've got enough goodness in you to vanquish the mightiest of devils."

Finley rewarded his faith with a thorough kiss. "I hope they catch her. Not just so she can be brought to justice for all the things she's done, but also so she can get help. I really don't think she was born evil. Circumstances just colored her view of life so that she couldn't see right from wrong."

"Maybe. Or maybe you need to take off your rose-colored glasses and accept that humans are flawed and not always good."

"Maybe," Finley murmured, as she rested her head against his shoulder and watched the dolphins lead them back to shore.

Officer Cabot was waiting for them at the pier when the ferry pulled into the dock. His partner was nowhere in sight. *Glad she isn't here. I don't have to try to wipe the I-told-you-so look off my face.*

While the others loaded into the vans, the Four Musketeers were called over for a conversation with Cabot. Finley minced no words when the conversation began. "Officer Cabot, we have been fully cooperative with your investigation. In fact, we have just given you information that allows you to arrest the suspect and gather the evidence necessary to bring her to trial," Finley stated.

Cabot started to interrupt but Finley cut him off. "In the course of this investigation, you and your partner have made my sister's wedding week a living hell. Something that cannot be remedied. Ever. We have a rehearsal and a dinner to attend in about an hour. For that, my sister will *not* be late. So, you have exactly fifteen minutes in which to take our statements and send us on our way. Or we will leave. And there is nothing you can do to stop us!"

Cabot stood silently, listening to Finley's edict before nodding slowly. "Officer Horton was pulled into another meeting as I was heading out here, but we can take your statements the day after to-morrow, if necessary. I know, Miss Blake, that you and Mr. Quinn will be leaving on your honeymoon, and we wouldn't do anything to interrupt that. So, the other officer and I will take yours right now, if that's okay." He smiled.

"Miss Garrett was apprehended just after you called," Cabot continued. "Turns out the attorney general's office had been tailing her as part of an investigation into fraud and bribery. They saw her packing up her car and were waiting for her on shore when the boat she used to get to and from the island slipped back into Sullivan's from Fort Sumter."

Whitt shook her head. "Bribery is the least of her worries now. She has murder and blackmail to account for!"

"And kidnapping, if you want to add our abduction to the list," Finley added.

"She kidnapped you?" Cabot turned to look at the sisters.

"At gunpoint," Whitt relayed. "She said the only reason she didn't add us to her body count was that she wouldn't have time to change out of her bloodstained clothes after she shot us! A real piece of work."

It took Cabot a few moments to regain his composure after that last revelation. After a few seconds, he signaled another officer over. "Officer Peters will take your statements, and then we will let you off to your festivities."

The house was much as it had been for the past week when the Four Musketeers walked in, freshened up and changed into their rehearsal dinner attire. The guys had forsaken their shorts and polos for linen pants and button-down shirts. David had opted for a white shirt and wheat-colored trousers, while Max went with a French blue shirt and sand-colored pants. They hadn't tried to coordinate, but Whitt's white halter sundress paired well with David's neutrals. Finley also played counterpoint to Max's blue with a navy pindot crepe jumpsuit.

The Four Musketeers entered the garden through the side gate. They saw that the crowd that normally populated Mama and Daddy's house had grown even larger, as those who wouldn't be attending the wedding were determined to get a view of Whitt's rehearsal. Mama had wisely asked the wedding planners to set up the chairs just as they would be for the wedding the next day. Almost every seat in the garden was occupied by family, friends, and neighbors.

"Does Mama plan on feeding all these people when we head off to the rehearsal dinner?" Seeing the people seated in the garden, Whitt's face registered her concern about the logistics of clearing the house in time for the dinner departure.

"Mrs. Calhoun has organized the church ladies to lead everyone over to the parish hall for a dinner that Mama and Daddy have catered." Finley grinned as her sister exhaled. She gifted Whitt a quick kiss. "Relax, baby sis. We've got it covered!"

"As always! I would expect no less from the Blake sisters!" announced a deep baritone voice with a subtle British accent.

"Evans!" Finley and Whitt squealed in tandem, as they greeted the tall, suave guest, who gathered a sister in each arm. His dark hair was flecked with more silver than there had been a year earlier in Jaipur, but his slate gray eyes still pierced with the same hawklike intensity and his throaty laugh still warmed the soul.

"When did you get in?" Whitt queried, after planting several kisses on his cheek.

"A couple of hours ago. I went to the house and let myself in and then came over here, per your instructions. Your mother has been feeding me ever since!" Evans chortled. He released the women and stepped back to take both in view. "Whitt, I can't wait to see you as a bride tomorrow! Thank you for including me in this celebration of life. We've seen enough death in our brief acquaintance."

Max stepped in to greet Evans, muttering, "You have no idea."

Evans's request for an explanation was cut short as Mama called everyone to attention. "Later," was all Max said as he moved toward the front and the rehearsal began.

Mama was grateful the rehearsal went off without any major glitches. The groomsmen all escorted the right bridesmaid, and Whitt remembered which side she was supposed to stand on. Finley remembered to grab Whitt's crepe paper bouquet even though

Max's sly, crooked smile kept distracting her. *What is he grinning for? I'll have to ask him over dinner. Hope he doesn't do that tomorrow. It's really confusing.*

Mama had recommended Frogmore Stew—a delectable meal-in-a-pot with shrimp, hot sausage, potatoes, and corn on the cob all simmered up in Old Bay and herbs—for the rehearsal dinner David's parents were hosting that evening. The wedding party and other guests boarded a small boat for the quick trip up the coast to a restaurant on the Isle of Palms. There, all the fixings for a great low-country boil were laid out. Pitchers of sunflowers adorned the red-and-white-checkered tables, which were lined up against the window that faced the water. Waiters wandered among the group, taking drink orders and setting out platters of pimento cheese and crab balls.

At dinner, Finley found herself sitting with David's mother, father, and sister, Tierney, the third of Whitt's bridesmaids. Tierney had arrived earlier in the afternoon, fresh from medical school exams. She'd blended well into the joking and goofing that had occurred during rehearsal, which was made easier by the fact that she and Whitt had met before. Finley decided she liked her. *A good thing, since we are going to be seeing a fair amount of each other over the years.*

David's parents peppered Finley with questions about her recent trip to Tanzania and Kenya as well as her other travels. Tierney mentioned that she was hoping to travel overseas once med school was over. Asia had a particular allure for her, especially the islands of Indonesia and Malaysia, so she was glad Whitt and David had decided to make Manila their home base, for now.

"I don't know how you do it! Both you and Whitt are always on the road. Thank goodness David and Max have jobs that allow some flexibility," Steve Quinn, David's father, remarked.

"Dad, you're assuming David and Max are the primary bread-winners!" Tierney interjected bemusedly. "That may not be the case.

These guys may be trailing behind these women for more than their good looks."

Finley chuckled at the last comment but said nothing.

"But what happens when the children come? Surely, you and your sister will settle into one place?" David's mother, Ellie, asked Finley, as if she could answer for her sister as well as herself.

"We'll have to make that decision when the time comes, I suppose," Finley diplomatically responded, but she already knew Whitt's answer—and so did David.

18

WHITT COULDN'T HAVE ASKED FOR a better day for a wedding in the South—clear blue skies cottoned with a few puffy white clouds, bright dappled sunshine, and a steady cooling breeze blowing off the water. *Clearly, Daddy remembered to bury the bourbon well in advance.*

Finley and Whitt had driven over to Mama and Daddy's with Charlie early that morning so they could have their hair and makeup done in time for the noon wedding. Whitt would have preferred a ten o'clock morning wedding with a luncheon, but Mama was adamant about a high noon nuptial with cocktails and an early dinner.

"Darling, the lighting is better at that time of day," Mama had advised. "You'll thank me later when you see the wedding pictures."

Whitt had conceded. She figured she had better things to think about than a two-hour difference in when she got married. It wasn't worth the argument. All she cared about was that she was indeed getting married.

The morning flew by and in no time, Whitt was standing at the back of the house, her arm looped through Daddy's, waiting for the music to start. All the guests were seated. Finley, Charlie, and Tierney stood near the willow reed arch that was festooned with sprays of flat eucalyptus, an assortment of succulents in dusty greens and grays, and varying hues of pink, magenta, and blush peonies. David stood, flanked by the priest and Max. He'd also asked his father and Dylan, a frat brother, to stand with him.

When the music, Bach's Air on the G String—selected by Whitt because of the cheeky play on words—started, all eyes turned to watch the bride. Finley instead glanced over at her soon-to-be brother-in-law. David's eyes were riveted on the woman who was to be his wife. His shoulders raised and then dropped as he exhaled deeply, a look of deep contentment gracing his face.

Whitt proved to be the vision of simple grace and serenity that she and Mama had imagined. The classic lines of the dress coupled with the lack of a wedding veil drew the guests' eyes to the radiant smile that illuminated her visage. *She's happy, truly happy. All her inner battles have been fought. David can breathe a sigh of relief,* Finley thought.

In the blink of an eye, the ceremony was over. Short and sweet, just like Whitt had wanted. David and Whitt were joined as one. As the first notes of a rondeau by Mouret were played, David took the hand of his beloved and led her up the aisle and into their future life together. No two people could have been happier.

Except for the matron of honor and the best man, perhaps, who followed them in the recessional. Max gently kissed the hand of his partner, Finley, as he escorted her from the garden. His grin, the lightness of his step, and the closeness with which he held her suggested that they, not Whitt and David, had just married. Daddy smiled in quiet recognition of the moment when they passed.

The photographer skillfully and quickly ushered guests out the garden gate and down the balloon- and flower-lined path that led between Mama and Daddy's place and the Davises' house, where the reception was being held. Mama had rightly let Finley take the lead in selecting a photographer for the event. Finley and Whitt had gone through the portfolios of at least a dozen photographers before selecting a young woman who was in her last year at the College of Charleston but already had her work picked up by *Vogue*, *Vanity Fair*, and *Rolling Stone* magazines.

With the formal poses captured, the wedding party moved to cocktails and dinner by the sea. Finley couldn't resist the urge to grab some candid shots of Whitt and David enjoying the first moments of wedded bliss and of Daisy trying so hard to offer her congratulations to the new bride—mindful of the "no paws on the silk" command that Whitt issued.

Once at Aunt Cora and Uncle John's house, Whitt and David, champagne firmly in hand, made the rounds throughout the cocktail hour and dinner, accepting the congratulations and best wishes of the gathered groups of intimate friends and family. Nessa and several other Blake cousins had arrived just minutes before the ceremony began, much to Daddy's consternation. Even that had failed to fluster Whitt, who greeted them all now with kisses and introductions to her new husband. Finley wondered whether Whitt had used the pageant girl's trick of lining her teeth with Vaseline to keep that permanent smile plastered on her face.

"She's glowing. I don't think I've ever seen her so happy. And with no smirk in sight." Evans had slipped alongside Finley as she stood looking out on the assembled gathering after dinner.

"She is! I don't know if I've ever seen her look so beautiful! Happiness makes the prettiest brides," Finley responded, her eyes fixed on the wedding couple as they moved to the dance floor for their first dance to the strains of *"Fly Me to the Moon."*

"Then Max must make you profoundly happy. You look simply stunning in that dress." Evans slid his gaze over her form in silent appreciation. "Do I get a dance at some point this evening?"

"You do indeed! I'm looking forward to it. You look like a man who knows his way around the dance floor," Finley remarked. "Can you shag?"

Evans's eyes widened in surprise. "I beg your pardon?"

Finley realized with amusement that a difference in meaning between American and British English had resulted in some confusion. What she had intended to suggest as a dance that resembled a slow, six-count hustle—the Carolina shag—had conveyed to Evans a slang term for salacious behavior.

"No, silly, in the South, a shag is a dance!" Finley explained.

Evans was visibly relieved. "I was worried there for a moment. I honestly didn't know the proper response. 'Yes, I can, but no, I won't' seemed most appropriate." He paused to smirk. "But it was such a tempting offer!"

Finley elbowed him playfully and redirected the conversation. "I know you say you're a confirmed bachelor, but I bet some special lady is going to get you to walk down the aisle at some point in the future," she teased.

"The only one who could have gotten me to take that step has been claimed." Evans smiled and gave Finley a side-glance. "Since she hasn't been cloned, as far as I know, I think I'll pass."

Finley remained silent for a few moments before giving him a sad smile.

Evans reached for her hand. "May I get that dance now?"

Finley responded by gently kissing his cheek as he led her to the dance floor for the first of what turned out to be a long evening of dancing between old friends. On several occasions during the evening, Max, Evans, and even Logan switched partners good-naturedly, to the confusion of some who didn't know the history that existed between Max and the other two men.

"Evans seems to be enjoying himself," Max observed when he and Finley took a breather at their table.

"He does. The ladies are quite taken with him. The rugged charm and the English accent. Though he says he doesn't have one!"

"Just like you say you don't have a Southern accent!" Max teased.

"I don't!" Finley retorted, until she realized that her "I" had come out as "Ah." She laughed. "Okay, point conceded!"

"I think it's a lovely accent. Uniquely yours. Please don't ever change," Max murmured.

It was late when Daddy pulled out the bottles of bourbon that had been buried in the garden to ensure good weather. Many of the guests had taken their leave shortly after Whitt and David had made their exit to an explosive display of fireworks and sparklers. Daddy had remembered Whitt's girlhood dream of being carried away from her wedding in a horse-drawn carriage like a storybook princess. So, David and Whitt were driven to their honeymoon suite in a white carriage pulled by a matched pair of black horses—just like in the movies.

The formalities concluded, the wedding party and a few close cousins from the Montgomery and Blake sides lounged at the tables closest to the sea. Brett had crawled under one of the tables and fallen asleep. Aunt Cora had covered her with a light blanket. Mama had gotten a fresh glass of champagne and taken a seat near where Daddy was pouring out fingers of bourbon. Odessa had kicked off her shoes and put her feet up on an adjacent chair.

"Katie Lynn, that was some shindig you and the general just threw!" Odessa accepted the glass of bourbon Daddy offered. "Which one is this, Ry?"

Daddy smiled when he saw Mama wince at being called her childhood nickname. He knew Odessa did it just to get under his wife's skin. He watched Mama take a sip of her champagne and adjust the skirt of the blush-colored, deeply V-necked evening dress she wore. He waited for her to say something witty in response to Odessa's jab, but she just sighed contentedly and looked out to sea.

Daddy returned his attention to the bourbon and Odessa. "This is the Pappy Van Winkle. You know I only pull out the good stuff when you come around!"

In time, the group grew quiet. Hema and Tierney sat on the edge of the pool, their feet dangling in the water, deep in discussion of some medical element that only they understood. Charlie and Evans shared a laugh over something Mooney said, while Ian gazed at her adoringly. Some, like Laine and Kirsten, had been wearied by the day's activities. Others, Mama and Daddy included, were quieted by the satisfaction the events brought. For Odessa, the champagne, wine, and bourbon had worked their magic and tugged heavily on her eyelids. Finley leaned back against Max. He wrapped his arms around her as they watched the scenarios play out.

"I know I told you earlier, but I feel this compelling need to say it again. You look amazing! The dress, your hair, everything!" Max kissed her hair and gently stroked her arm. "You have this astounding ability to keep making me fall deeper and deeper in love with you, over and over again. Don't know whether you're aware of it."

"I wasn't, but thank you for revealing my secret power!" Finley chortled at Max's effusiveness. "You look quite dashing yourself. There were several of my cousins who would have gladly taken you home."

"Oh, they would've returned me by morning. My snoring would've had them running for the hills!"

"It's not that bad. Just reminds me of the rumble of a midnight train!" Finley teased. She looked over at Mama, who had assumed a similar position in Daddy's arms. "I think Mama is glad Albertine skipped the wedding. It would have been awkward given what she told Mama and Lael's arrest."

"Did Lael ever say why she did all that she did?" Max asked. "A really disturbed woman."

"She gave reasons, but they really didn't explain why she did it. Beyond it being something that she did because she could. Like it was game. Taking money, blackmailing people, even killing Tommy. So sad."

"Well, it's over. Maybe we can get in some sightseeing before we head home. Then, we need to decide where we're going next."

"Later. Let's just enjoy some slow time before we get back on the hamster wheel!"

With that, Max pulled her fully into his lap and kissed her until she went weak in his arms.

Finley and Max were slow to get up the next morning. They could smell coffee brewing and hear the bustling as those in the house packed up and prepared to leave for the airport. Evans was the first out the door, rushing for a flight to Atlanta and then onward to Bangkok and goodness knew where else. He shared a taxi to the airport with Mooney and Ian, who were flying to Los Angeles for another friend's wedding the following week.

"I barely got a chance to say a word to you," Mooney whined to Finley, as she stepped into the waiting cab. "You have to book a trip to the city, so we can catch up. I have so much I need to fill you in on!" *Another wedding?* Finley wondered.

The Blake cousins stopped in for a quick farewell before caravanning up the coast to Virginia.

"Do you think it's too early to start that child on therapy?" Max asked earnestly when they had pulled away.

"Max! There is nothing wrong with that child that an earlier bedtime won't cure," Finley admonished before taking a last look at the little face pressed against the glass and waving a cheery goodbye. *Let's hope!*

The next out the door were Hema and Logan, who were giving Charlie a ride to Washington, DC on the "private" before jetting up to Maine for the weekend. Logan had confided to Finley that he'd decided on Maine as the place to pop the question, in part because it was so quintessentially American and because he had found a picture of Kennebunkport tucked away in Hema's calendar. He didn't know whether it was because Maine was on her bucket list of places to visit or because she just liked the picture. Whatever the reason, it seemed an ideal backdrop for a picture-perfect proposal.

"I know she would say yes wherever you decided to ask her. Just remember my invitation to the wedding!" Finley had teased.

Kirsten and Reid loaded up the minivan shortly after Logan and his crew left. "We should have been out of here an hour ago.

My mother is holding lunch for us, I know. But all the vapor from the wine and champagne last night got me drunk, so I decided to take it easy this morning."

Reid just shook his head at his wife's silliness as he helped her into the car and buckled her seatbelt for her. "When you see us next time, we will have babies in tow!" Reid declared, sliding into the driver's seat. "Life will never be the same!"

"Good luck!" Max called out as they drove away.

He turned to Finley, who stood waving until the van turned the corner. "How many babies do you want?"

"What?" Finley paused, momentarily shocked. "Where did that come from?"

"I was just thinking, seeing Kirsten pregnant with two. When she said she was done after these two, Reid looked like he had other plans in that regard. Clearly, there's going to be some negotiating going on between those two. So, I thought I'd ask."

Finley took Max's hand and led him into the house. "That's a pretty heavy question to ask a girl before she's had coffee. Can I respond after I've had a cup?"

Max answered by opening the door to the deck and pool. "Grab a seat, and I'll be right out with coffee."

In minutes, Max came out with a small tray filled with two mugs of coffee and a plate of cinnamon biscuits. "Thought the biscuits would give you food for thought."

The two sat in comfortable silence as they sipped their coffee and nibbled their biscuits. It was almost ten minutes before either spoke.

"Two or three," Finley finally stated.

Max glanced at her briefly and smiled. "If three, more girls than boys—if you can indeed arrange that."

"I too have a preference for little girls. But who knows what we'll have. Just pray that they're healthy," Finley murmured, the last words fading into a whisper.

Max raised her hand to his lips and kissed it. They returned to sipping their coffee in silence.

Finley and Max were getting ready to leave for Mama and Daddy's when Officer Cabot pulled up. He took his time getting out of the car.

After a few minutes of waiting for him to come to the door, Finley, perturbed at having to delay her departure, exited the house with Max in tow and began to lock up. Seeing that the two were getting ready to leave, Cabot got out of the car and approached them.

"Sorry to disturb you on a Sunday. Hope the wedding went well." Cabot had removed his hat and was circling the band with his hand.

"Where's your partner today?" Finley inquired, mainly to start the conversation she hoped would end quickly.

Cabot looked down at his hat sheepishly. "That's what I wanted to talk to you about. When I stopped by the other day, I mentioned that Horton had been called into the captain's office just as I was leaving. I didn't know why. Well, turns out Horton and your cousin, Miss Garrett, were sorority sisters."

"And?" Finley pressed Cabot to get to the point.

"And Horton knew that Miss Garrett was on the take with a lot of people here in the city. Still, she didn't report it or do anything to stop it. In fact, Miss Garrett was slipping some of the money to Horton. Internal Affairs is investigating after Miss Garrett outed Horton."

He continued to stare at his hat. "Horton was the one who kept insisting your sister and her fiancé had something to do with Mr. Pierce's death. I don't know what she planned to do, maybe plant something, but it's clear now that she knew at the time that your cousin was involved in Mr. Pierce's death. She purposely interfered with an investigation. I wanted to apologize for putting your sister through that, especially just before her wedding."

Finley reached out and touched the young man's shoulder. "You thought you were doing your job. No harm done in the end."

When Cabot drove off, Finley and Max hopped in the car and headed to Sullivan's. The trip over the bridge barely took fifteen minutes without the weekday traffic. Mama and Daddy were out back, lazing by the pool, when Finley and Max slipped through the gate. Daisy was the first to see them and took off across the lawn toward them. Finley's silent command brought the young dog to a stop. Daisy dropped down beside Finley and waited for the next command. Instead, she got a release and a belly rub.

"You're going to ruin my dog with all that spoiling, girl!" Daddy greeted Finley with a kiss and hug before turning to shake Max's hand. "What kept you so long? Your mama was getting ready to send out the National Guard for you. You texted saying you were on your way a while ago."

Max explained the morning of long goodbyes and the visit from Officer Cabot.

"Horton had her hand in the till, too! Good gracious. Your mama is going to feel vindicated." Daddy chuckled as they headed toward where Mama was sitting. "She never did like that woman."

Max smiled wryly. "She had a partner there. Neither did Fin."

The afternoon slipped into evening as they all shared their favorite memories of the previous week. Every detail of the wedding, from the flowers and balloons to the bubbles and fireworks and even the birdseed pouches, had been touches that made Whitt's nuptials special. After each mention, Daddy simply said, "That's what your mama wanted." Mama lovingly patted his cheek in response.

As the night went on, Daddy pulled out the rest of the Van Winkle and poured fingers all around. Not as bold in flavor as the Taylor Mash had been, the Van Winkle made up for its more subtle flavor with a roundness and smoothness that had Max closing his eyes in appreciation.

"Like that, do you? How does it match up against the single malts you're so fond of?" Daddy questioned, taking a mouthful of the amber liquid.

"Quite favorably." Max nodded. "I may actually come to like this better!"

"Really? You sure you aren't just saying that because you're with a Southern woman?"

Max responded with a quick glance at Finley and a lopsided grin.

"What we don't do for the love of a Southern girl!" Daddy patted his son-in-law on the back.

Later that night, as Finley and Max sat in bed talking about the life decisions they needed to make in the next several months—about what assignments to take next and where to live—the question of "home" came up again.

"Does it bother you to be so transient?" Max queried. "I mean, we have the place in Chelsea, but we're rarely there. And it sounds like we'll be there even less over the next year. Do you want to settle down, stay put for a while? If you want, we can work out of New York so you can be closer to your family." *And yours, if you want to reconnect*, Finley considered saying, but she kept her thoughts to herself.

Finley had been thinking about home and what it meant since Max had raised the question weeks before. She realized that the conversations had always been focused on a place. Whether New York or London felt more like home. Whether she could live in DC or Charleston. What she finally acknowledged that night was that she never really felt untethered because she had always felt grounded in family—Mama and Daddy, Whitt, and now David. And Max. That was where she now found peace, stability, and serenity. It was less a place than a state of mind.

Finley reached out and touched Max's face. She slowly shook her head. "No need to decide on one place, unless you really want to. Home is wherever my soul feels centered. That can be any place in world, quite truthfully. Sounds hokey, but I feel most centered when I'm with you." She smiled. "You're my home."

The End

If you enjoyed this book and want to learn
more about Finley and Whitt Blake
join our mailing list at www.mcarterfielding.com or
drop me a line at carter.fielding6554@gmail.com.
I'd love to hear from you.
Talk soon!

Read on to get a sneak peek at the next book in
the Blake Sisters Travel Mystery series

A Blake Sisters Travel Mystery
Book 5
Murder at the Summit

Carter Fielding

CHAPTER 1

DAVID QUINN AND MAX DAVIES, the spouses of Whitt Blake and her sister Finley, were as giddy-excited about their diving schedule as two boys heading out on their first fishing trip. Their guide had met the two at the Puerta Princesa Hotel shortly after the Four Musketeers, as the foursome called themselves when together, arrived in Palawan. The crew had opted for the early flight from Manila into Puerto Princesa that put them into Palawan mid-morning.

The time in Manila had gone quickly. Too quickly. David had barely pulled the car into the drive of the new house in Makati Whitt and David had moved into after their marriage before the sisters were chattering like magpies. David and Max had just rolled their eyes and stepped aside. The` four-bedroom bungalow was more spacious than the chic high-rise apartment Whitt had called home for several years before her marriage. Room for Whitt and David to each have a home office as well as a guest room. The new house also had a yard, an important feature given their new addition.

A staccato of tiny, high-pitched barks had prompted Finley to peer around the door into a small, partitioned area. "What's that sound?" she had asked as she investigated. Neither Whitt nor David responded, but instead cast side glances at each other.

"Did you two get a dog?" Max inquired just as Finley reached the half-gate and peered over.

Finley came around the ante-room corner carrying a caramel-colored round of fur that was alternating between licking her face and barking warnings. "Is it a he or a she?" Finley lifted the fluff ball up to check its sex.

David leaned against the counter as both Max and Finley cuddled with the Golden Retriever puppy snuggled in Finley's arms. "Delilah's a little girl. I got her as a wedding present for Whitt. We got kind of used to having Daisy Duke around and thought it would be a nice addition to our household." Daisy Duke was their daddy's dog in Charleston. They had all fallen in love with her while they were all there preparing for Whitt and David's wedding.

"How old? " Max inquired.

"Almost nine weeks. Whitt says she's always been partial to females, and she likes the reddish ones. Delilah has both, so she became ours!" David seemed pleased with his decision.

Later that afternoon, Finley stepped out of the shower to find her tall muscular partner stretched out on the floor, napping, with Delilah curled comfortably on his chest. The ensuing conversation had been enlightening for her.

"Has she been here all the while?" Max had awoken and given the still sleeping puppy a nuzzle.

"The two of you were curled up asleep the whole time. I kept checking to be sure she hadn't had an accident and she was dead to the world on your chest!" Finley had said.

"You think our babies will do that?" Max had looked up from the puppy and held Finley's eye. Lately he had been asking about babies and raising children. He was clearly signaling that he was ready. But was she?

"I think they will, when they feel safe and secure," Finley had replied before touching his cheek gently. "You'd better get dressed. We have dinner in another hour or so. Whitt says her friends have been dying to meet us!"

"I would be careful using the word "dying" when you two sisters are together! It can be dangerous!" Max teased.

While Max played it off as a joke, it did seem that whenever the sisters were together there was murder involved. Whether in Tangier, Galle, Jaipur, or Charleston, if Finley and Whitt were together, something deadly was bound to happen. And yet David and Max had pledged themselves to these sisters anyway. Six months ago, almost to the day, Whitt and David had become husband and wife. A year before that, Max and Finley had committed to each other forever, their version of "committed permanence without marriage", in deference to Max's aversion to the institution.

"Fin," Max had called to her softly as she reached the door. "I love you. I realized I hadn't said it today and I try to say it at least once daily, so you'll know! I don't ever want you to have to guess."

Finley had wondered whether his parents' complicated relationship had been the reason for the practice. Whatever the reason, she liked it. "I love you more!" was all she had said as she slipped out the door.

Twilight had settled in when the Four Musketeers arrived at Blackbird, a fashionable restaurant in Makati, housed in an art deco space that had been the international airport in the 1930s. The stark white two-story interior of the restaurant, with its floor to ceiling, dark-wood encased windows and dramatic towering floral arrangements, made a statement. Several of the group from the bank where Whitt worked had arrived by the time Whitt and the others walked in. Finley had heard so much about Whitt's bank friends--— Aliyan and Saskia, Rob and Amiko, and Francisco and Caroline, Monica and Jay. Charlie, Whitt's best friend in Manila, rounded out the group, even though she didn't work at the bank.

"You guys heading to Palawan?" Rob had poured himself another glass of wine and leaned back against the chair, his arm resting around Amiko's shoulders. "The diving is some of the best in the world. David knows!"

David nodded. "Hoping to get the ladies to join us for at least some snorkeling before they head up to the Summit. In any event,

Max and I are heading out on a charter—El Nido and a few other spots that this guy says are good."

Caroline sat up and stared at Whitt. "You're going to the Summit? How did you swing that? The waitlist for that place is a mile long!"

Monica agreed. "Daniella, Mark's wife, had her name on the list for almost six months before she finally got in. She said the specialized treatments were well worth it, though. They have an anti-gravity capsule. Supposed to take years off your face!" Mark was another of their colleagues at the bank.

Whitt laughed, "Daniella isn't even thirty. If she gets any more years taken off, she'll be back in diapers! I'll be staying away from that one."

Whitt continued, "No big secret to getting in. I won four days for two at the Summit at the Children's Welfare benefit gala. And this is the weekend. Then Finley got an assignment to write about the best spas in Asia…"

Finley interjected, "A difficult mission but someone had to make the sacrifice!"

"David didn't want to go, so Charlie volunteered…"

"What I don't do for my friends!" Charlie giggled.

After the consultation with the diving guide, the foursome settled in their rooms in Puerto Princesa, changed into their swimsuits and grabbed snorkeling gear from the activities hut. Finley and Whitt agreed to snorkeling before lunch, but neither wanted to spend the full day diving. Whitt made it clear that she had set aside the afternoon for shopping, Finley's least favorite sport, before they were picked up for the drive to the Summit early the next morning. David shook his head slightly at his wife's proposed round of shopping therapy and got ready to say something before Finley interrupted.

"So where did the diving guide say y'all were going to go?" Finley directed her gaze at Max, signaling him to help her change the subject before David got himself into hot water. Max picked up the cue and described the course that had been charted for the "seafari" they were embarking on.

"We'll do the hot spots like the reefs off Puerto Princesa as well as El Nido before we head up to Coron." Max's finger sketched an imaginary route up the coast. Finley pictured the map of Palawan in her mind and saw the sailboat the men had chartered following the course north and then slightly east. "And it looks like we are going to Tubbataha!"

The reef Max mentioned was reputed to be one of the most beautiful in all of the Philippines, if not the world. Designated a UNESCO World Heritage Site, the reef was part of the Cagayancillo National Marine Park. While David had hoped to be able to dive the challenging spot, he wasn't sure that they would have time to make the 12-hour trip out and back, as well as decompress, in time to make their flight to Manila. The addition of a day to the itinerary had made the dive possible.

"Thanks for being willing to take the extra time so we could do Tubbataha." David reached and took a piece of bacon from Whitt's plate, giving her a chunk of papaya in exchange.

"As if they really have to suffer, David!" Max gave Finley a sly grin. "Our wives get an extra day of massages that we agreed to pay for!"

Finley smiled. She had begun to like it now when Max called her his wife, notwithstanding their less than formal marital arrangement. He had taken to addressing her as such shortly after their commitment in London almost a year and a half ago. It had gotten her in trouble though when he went so far as to intimate to relatives at Whitt and David's wedding that they were married. She had had to explain to him that in the South, skipping the big wedding, especially if you had the means, generally led to speculation about whether the bride was already with child.

Finley looked at her sister nestled in David's arms and saw the same contentment in Whitt that she felt with Max. There was a time Whitt had sworn she would never get married. And yet now, here she was, married and very much in love. "When does Charlie arrive?" Finely asked.

"Tomorrow morning. She's taking the same flight that we were on, but she's coming straight to the Summit," Whitt replied.

"Well, I, for one, am going to take advantage of the sun this afternoon, while these ladies head out shopping." Max angled his body closer to Finley on the banquette as he spoke. "And then I am going to recommend that we take these beautiful women out for a special dinner before we part ways. As much as I am looking forward to the time at sea, I'm going to miss my lady love."

Finley was a bit surprised by Max's sentimentality. Normally, the man was the epitome of stoicism. For the longest, she had assumed that only she had been torn up by their parting in Tangier many years ago. Every indication was that Max had moved on after she left. A chance meeting in that city a few years later revealed that nothing could have been further from the truth. Max too had been destroyed by their break-up but had shown it in ways not apparent to most. More recently, however, he had loosened his reserve and talked more openly, with deep affection. Finley had to admit that as much as she liked it, it took a little getting used to.

It took more than a little browsing to get Whitt "shopped out" after they left the guys and headed to the shops. After the ninth store, Finley sat down in the little courtyard that connected several of the shops to rest her feet. "Give me your bags, Whitt. I'll sit here while you finish. I refuse to walk anymore!"

Finley laughed as Whitt scurried off to the next artisan's shop. Any excuse to shop was good enough for Whitt. She had inherited Mama's shopping gene, no doubt. It didn't matter where they were in the world. Whitt was going to find the best shops and exhaust their inventory before she left. That said, she always came back with exquisite finds!

"Did you see that?" Whitt came back and sat beside Finley on the bench. She directed her eyes toward a large entourage of people clustered around a petite, stylishly dressed woman. "That's Angie Pineda, she was a former Miss International. That was almost 20 years ago but she is really revered here. Still has quite a few local endorsements."

She peered over her shoulder and nodded in the direction of something behind her. "You see that tall Indian guy with the Anglo chick on his arm? That's Arun Mehta, the big Bollywood star, Remember, he was lead in that movie, *Remembrance*, you saw with Max in Delhi? Like night and day how they are traveling. Arun trying to keep his head down and not be seen. And Miss International trying to attract as much attention as she can get!"

"When his star wanes, he'll probably do the same!" Finley remarked scanning the crowd for other glitterati. "Anyone else rich and famous that I missed?"

"None that I can see, but let's grab a glass of wine at Tomaso's and see who else we can spot. I was told that is the go-to spot for 'star-gazing' on the island." Whitt gathered up her multitude of bags and started toward to main street. "That's where the Hong Kong, and occasionally some American, movie stars hang out, so who knows who we will see!"

Puerto Princesa hadn't struck Finley as the type of place any movie star worth his salt would go. While the location on the water was appealing, there wasn't much to see. A few hotels, a cluster or two of shops and a sprinkling of restaurants, both in town and along the seafront. Finley had yet to see what she would call a five-star hotel, but then she had only just arrived.

The waiter at Tomaso's showed them to an outside table tucked away on the side of the broad veranda. The table's location gave them a charmed view of the water—and the other guests, of which there were quite a few. Parts of Miss International's entourage had planted themselves at a large table in the center of the restaurant. Miss International herself, however, was nowhere to be seen.

Finley took a sip of her wine and changed the subject to their stay at the Summit. "What treatments are you going to get done? I tried a seaweed wrap when I was in Thailand and liked it. Maybe I'll do that again."

"I listed out several things I want to try. The diagnostic scan they do seemed pretty interesting. And some of the hydrotherapy sessions sounded relaxing." Whitt picked up an olive and popped it into her mouth.

"I'm going to stick to the spa and yoga options. The description of some of the other treatments verged on proctology, if you asked me!"

At Finley's last comment, Whitt almost spit the olive pit across the room. "You're incorrigible!"

"Well, it's true! Did you read the flyers carefully? They are talking about probing and prodding places that I'd just as soon leave alone." Finley cast a side glance at her sister. "Since when did you get so adventurous?"

"Since I won this trip! It's not often that you get to try this stuff out all expenses paid!" Whitt sprang to her feet. "We'd better settle our bill and get back. I almost forgot. We have dinner with the boys tonight!"

When the alarm went off at 4 am the next morning, Finley wanted to turn over and go back to sleep. The foursome had drunk their way well into the morning. However, powered by adrenaline, Max had jumped out of bed and bolted for the shower as soon as the alarm rang. In no time, he was dressed and ready to head down to grab the breakfast packs the hotel had made for them.

Finley slowly pulled on a sundress and ran a brush through her hair before heading off to the bathroom to brush her teeth.

"This is as good as it gets!" she announced as she staggered sleepily back into the room. She leaned against the door with her eyes closed. "This is inhumane! Are you guys getting up this early every morning?"

Max walked over and pulled her away from the wall and into his arms. "My beautiful Sleeping Beauty! How I am going to miss you!" He kissed her eyelids, her forehead and her nose before engaging her lips with a kiss so thorough that Finley hung in Max's arms limply when they pulled apart.

"That was nice! Very nice! I think I like being missed!" Finley drawled lazily as she reached up and drew Max to her again. "I'm going to miss you, too!"

Later, when the guys had been loaded into the car that would take them to the boat for their trip and departed, Whitt and Finley headed back upstairs. Their car to the Summit wouldn't arrive for another few hours.

"You headed back to bed?" Whitt asked when they reached the doors to their respective rooms.

Finley shook her head. "Nope. I was going to shower and then go get coffee out by the water."

"Good idea. I'll join you. And I'll call the resort and ask the car to come early!"

Just over an hour later, a black Range Rover from the Summit pulled up in front of the hotel. The driver placed their luggage in the back and helped the sisters take their seats.

"Welcome to the Summit. I am sure you will enjoy your stay. If there is anything I can get for you before we begin the short ride up the hill, please let me know. There is water in the fold-down arm rest and the International New York Times and Financial Times are in the seat pocket." He paused to see if Finley and Whitt had any immediate needs. "If not, we will be on our way."

And with that the trip to the Summit began. In no time, the bustle of the town proper was forgotten amidst a forested area that ended at a stone gate which opened to a long palm-lined lane. At the end of the lane was a two-story, thatched wooden edifice with pillars of stone that matched the entry gate. All around verdant palms, interspersed among strategically placed pools, danced a welcome in the morning breeze.

"Welcome to the Summit. I hope Jun made your trip enjoyable!" A bright-faced young woman in a skirt and beautifully embroidered blouse made of sheer *pinya* fibers greeted them at a flower-strewn entrance. The air smelled of sandalwood and lemongrass. "My name is Dalisay. I am here throughout your stay to ensure that it is a good one and that you come back to visit us again soon."

Whitt and Finley followed the woman inside the reception area as the driver helped the bellman load the bags onto a cart for the ride to their villa. The reception offered a postcard-worthy impression. The beamed ceiling soared into a steep pitch that was lined with raffia matting. Four large hewn trees acted as supporting posts. Three of the building walls were open to the carefully sculpted landscaping. Around the floor areas, bentwood and rattan chairs were arranged in careful clusters, separated by tree-trunk tables polished to a natural sheen.

"Nimoy will take care of your bags while we orient you to the property and all that it has to offer. As I mentioned, my name is Dalisay and I will be our guide throughout your stay. I understand that another guest will be joining you shortly. When she arrives, we will escort her to your villa. In the meantime, let me acquaint you with the resort."

By the time, Finley and Whitt arrived at the room after their tour, they had already signed up for an afternoon yoga class to ease them into the spa life. No sooner had they unpacked than they heard a faint knocking on the villa front door.

"Charlie!" Whitt acted as the official greeter, pulling her friend into the entryway and pointing the way to Charlie's room for the porter carrying her bag. "Did you just get in?"

"About fifteen minutes ago. And then I went through the greeting ritual. You would have thought as many times as I have been here, they would have dispensed with the formalities and just brought me to the room. In any event, I'm in the same yoga class you signed up for."

Charlie walked over to the open patio terrace and breathed in. "This is what you come here for! Hear that? Silence! Absolute silence!"

A petite strawberry blonde, Charlie had been Whitt's best friend since moving to the Philippines. The director of a no-kill animal shelter, Charlie had become like a second sister since Whitt's wedding. In Charleston, she had seen the sisters in action, when they worked to solve the mystery of a body found in the Airbnb in which they were staying. Now she stood, eyes closed, taking in the tranquility that surrounded her. She turned to give both Whitt and Finley a hug. "Now you may break my reverie! What time did you guys arrive?" she asked.

"Maybe thirty` minutes before you did! The guys left at the crack of dawn, and Whitt and I lazed about with coffee on the beach until we headed up here." Finley relayed.

"Have you guys unpacked? I want a walk before I deal with that task. You up for it?" Charlie suggested. "It's been a tough week and I need to decompress, if you guys don't mind."

The sisters quickly nodded, and the threesome struck out along the manicured paths that led through the grounds. "Looks pretty quiet. I guess it's still early, though. Most of the guests will check in tonight for the weekend." Finley observed.

"Gosh! I guess it is only ten o'clock! The morning is still young!" Whitt pointed to a sign, turning to Charlie. "Let's go to the water-fall! Do you know where it is?"

Charlie nodded and led the way. The path narrowed as they wound their way through the lush vegetation toward the falls. Fallen leaves and decaying palm fronds blackened the pebbles and coconut mulch that covered the way, enlightened only by periodic shards of sunlight that cut through the canopy.

They heard the rush of the water and felt the mist from the spray long before they arrived at the falls itself. As they came around a large boulder, the beauty of the falls met them full-face.

"Oh, my goodness, this is spectacular!" Finley gushed, pulling her camera from her backpack. "Who would have thought you would have your own private falls tucked back here?"

She moved forward, never taking her eye from the viewfinder or her finger from the shutter. After shooting several frames, Finley shifted to look back at her sister and friend who had ceased talking. She assumed they, like her, were silenced by the magnificent view.

"Isn't this amazing?" Finley started to say. She stopped short. The stunned looks on the faces of Charlie and Whitt said something else. She followed their line of sight and finally understood their reaction.

There on the surface of the pool, at the foot of the falls, half-hidden in the flowering vines that covered the face of the waterfall, was the form of a young woman. At first, Finley thought she was just floating on her back. But when she failed to move after several minutes, Finley realized what Whitt and Charlie already knew. The poor woman was dead.